ROSE OF SKIBBEREEN

BOOK 5: ROSIE

By John McDonnell

Copyright © 2014 John McDonnell

ISBN-13: 9798651501427

Discover other titles at John McDonnell's Amazon page:
amazon.com/author/johnmcdonnell

INTRODUCTION

This is Book Five in the series about Rose Sullivan from Skibbereen, Ireland. I wrote these books because of an old photograph of a teenage girl in a family album. The photograph was of my mother's grandmother, whose name was Kate Burchill. Kate was born on a farm in Skibbereen, County Cork, Ireland. She took a ship to Philadelphia in 1880, looking for a better life, and she never went back to Ireland, which meant she never saw her family for the rest of her days (and she lived 60 more years).

But my great-grandmother's life was just the starting point of this saga. What I soon learned in Book One was that "Rose of Skibbereen" was developing a life of its own. The story grew in unexpected ways and went off in directions I never anticipated. The characters seemed to have a life of their own, and I followed along after them writing down their story. It has been a great joy for me to see how this story developed, and I hope you are enjoying it also.

It's not over yet!

PROLOGUE

This is Book Five in the "Rose Of Skibbereen" series, a group of fictional stories about the family of Rose Sullivan from Skibbereen, County Cork, Ireland. Here is a synopsis of the story so far:

Book One. Rose Sullivan from Skibbereen sails to America in 1880 to work as a domestic servant, so she can send money back to her impoverished family in Ireland. The night before she sails she meets a handsome young man named Sean McCarthy, who kisses her and then leaves. Rose never forgets him, and she meets him five years later in Philadelphia, where they both are working for the same wealthy family, the Lancasters. Rose doesn't know that Sean killed a British officer in Ireland, and he'd fled to America and changed his name to Peter Morley. When he meets Rose he never tells her why he changed his name or anything about the murder. They get married and have three sons: Tim, Paul, and Willy.

Book Two. It starts in 1900, when Peter (Sean) disappears on New Year's Day. He was feeling trapped in his marriage to Rose and he'd fallen in love with an English girl in Philadelphia named Edith Jones. Now Sean makes up another identity. He tells Edith his name is James Francis, and reveals nothing about his marriage to Rose. He marries Edith and has two children with her, Mercy and John. He gets a job as a driver for Siegmund Lubin, an early 20th century movie director in Philadelphia, and picks up some bit parts in Lubin's movies. He has a roving eye, and soon he cheats on Edith with actresses in Lubin's films. Edith discovers this in 1912 when she surprises James with a visit to the set of a movie he's in. She has brought Mercy and John, her two children with him, and they see his betrayal. Edith leaves him then.

Meanwhile, Rose's sons Tim and Paul go to work at a paper mill, and Paul falls in love with Lucy, the daughter of the owner of the mill. Paul marries Lucy, works hard, and has two children, Rosie and Billy. Paul's brother Willy dies in an accident as a young man, and Tim dies in 1930 from alcoholism. Shortly after that Sean/Peter/James dies of a heart attack on the porch of Paul's house, where he has come to apologize for leaving Rose as a young man. Paul finds out about his father's other wife, Edith, and he locates her and tells her about the death of her husband. It is the first time she learns her husband's history -- that he was married to Rose and had three sons with her.

Book Three. It starts in 1935. Rose has reunited with Martin Lancaster, son of the family she worked for as a young woman, a man who has always loved her, and they are now married. Her son Paul now owns the paper mill, and appears to be a rich man. He comes under the influence of American Nazi sympathizers, though, and becomes active in their organization as a speaker. His company is struggling in the Depression, and he is secretly embezzling money from it. Eventually he goes to prison for tax fraud, to the shame of his family. Rosie, his daughter, a rebellious girl, sneaks out to sing with a big band orchestra at a club in Philadelphia, and meets an English naval officer named James Charlesworth. She has an affair with him, and becomes pregnant. It is now the end of World War II, and Charlesworth tells Rosie he is going home to England to his wife and children. Rosie is on the verge of suicide and is about to jump off a bridge, but a policeman talks her out of it. Edith has fallen in love with a Jewish man and moved to Israel. Her daughter Mercy has moved to California. Her son John died during World War II. Rose dies at the age of 98 in 1960, just after John F. Kennedy is elected President.

Book Four. It starts in 1961. Rosie is living in South Philadelphia with her son Pete. She loves to sing, and she gets involved in the early doo-wop scene, mentoring a singer and his vocal group. Rosie is passionate and mercurial, and she also has psychic ability. Her judgment is poor, however. She angers a local mobster and has to leave town quickly. She moves to London just before the Beatles become popular, and she gets involved in the Swinging Sixties music scene in London as the assistant to a talent agent. She stays ten years, but her absence is traumatic for her son Pete, whom she left in Philadelphia with her parents, Paul and Lucy. Pete gets into trouble in school, and then joins the Army at seventeen and is sent to Vietnam, where he is wounded in combat.

Mercy comes back to Philadelphia on a mission to find old silent films from Siegmund Lubin, and she meets Lorenzo, a cab driver she falls in love with. Rosie reunites with James Charlesworth in London, and now he wants to leave his wife for her. She refuses, and comes back to Philadelphia in 1970. Pete meets Betty, an African American woman who was the girlfriend of a soldier he knew in Vietnam. The soldier was killed in combat, and Pete visits Betty to deliver mementoes from her dead boyfriend. Pete falls in love with Betty. The book ends in 1976.

Book Five starts in 1979.

CHAPTER ONE

November 1979

Rosie hadn't had this dream in awhile, but she remembered being here before. She was at the top of a long ridge that was like the crest of a wave, and she was looking down on a valley that had a stream running at the bottom of it. There were clumps of mist clinging to the low ground, and she could see the sun glinting through wisps of clouds on the mountain at the other side of the valley.

And there was the most beautiful music playing! It wafted up from the valley like a sweet aroma, from instruments that she could not identify exactly. Perhaps a violin or two, some kind of bagpipe, a tin whistle. A chorus of voices behind a high, aching voice that was lamenting something. It was sad but sweet, and she wanted to hear more of it.

As before, she found herself running down the hillside to the cluster of trees by the stream, which is where the music was coming from. She had to get down there and see who was playing it, find out for once what this strange, sweet music meant, who was behind it.

She got closer, halfway down the hillside, with the spring grass smell in her nose and the sun on her cheeks, and the sky fighting between dark and light, mist and clarity. She was closer, closer; it seemed that this time she would finally get there. . .

And then she was awake once again, with the gnawing feeling of loss inside, like so many times before. She stared up at the white ceiling of her bedroom, saw the pattern of the roses on her wallpaper, and heard the sounds of the cars going by on the street outside.

Why did this happen again? She hadn't dreamed that dream in awhile, but now it was back, with the same result.

Something is missing in my life, she thought. The dream is telling me there is something missing. But what?

And then she heard the knocking on the door downstairs. It was an insistent rapping, three raps then a pause, and then three more raps. On and on it went, as if the person knew she was inside and would not stop until she opened the door.

She looked at the clock radio on the stand next to her bed. It said 8:30. The record store didn't open until 10:00, so why was someone knocking on the door?

It was probably another crazy oldies collector. She had dealt with a number of these fanatics since she and Dittybopper opened the store a year ago, guys who were obsessed with collecting old 45 records or 78 LPs, and they came around all the time with their greedy eyes, pawing the records in the bins and trying to find a record by some obscure group of teenaged a capella singers from 1954, some group that only released a couple of records and then faded into obscurity.

Oldies were starting to get popular nationally, not just here in Philadelphia, and these collectors were looking to make a killing. The prices of these 45s had gone up steadily in the last couple of years, and the crazy fanatics had come out of the woodwork.

Rap, rap, rap!

Rosie got out of bed and fumbled around on the floor, looking for her jeans. She slept in only a t-shirt and underwear, and once she found her jeans crumpled up on the floor next to an empty wine bottle she pulled them on, then wormed her feet into flip flops and looked at herself in the mirror.

She saw a middle aged lady, with bags under her somewhat bloodshot eyes, brown hair with gray roots showing, and a bit too much stomach hanging over the waistband of her jeans.

You look every bit your age, she thought. You're 52 and selling oldies records to weird guys who can't look you in the eye and would sell their own grandmother to the Mafia to get their greasy hands on a mint condition Danny And The Juniors version of "Pony Express".

Rap, rap rap!

"Okay," she yelled in the direction of the nearest window, which was open a crack. "Back off, pal. I'm coming!"

She found her way down the stairs blearily to the office in the back of the store, then unlocked the door and went through the aisles of record bins to the front of the store.

As she suspected it was a man at the door, and he looked strange. He had longish hair, thick glasses, and ill-fitting clothes. His pale skin looked like he spent a lot of time indoors.

She unlocked the door and opened it just a crack, enough to say, "We don't open till 10, mister. You can come back later."

"No, please!" he said. "I drove all the way here from Bucks County. I don't get the car much, and this is a big deal for me. I'm looking to sell a record. It's important, please, can I come in?"

Rosie wanted to tell him to go away, because part of her worried that he was some kind of loony, but his eyes looked gentle and she felt sorry for him. He probably didn't have much else in his life besides record collecting.

"Please?" he said again. "I won't stay long. I just want to find out if you're interested in this. It's a mint condition record. My mother died a month ago, and I found all these old records in her attic. I think some of them are valuable. You could make a lot of money on these!"

Rosie had heard that story before, from wild-eyed record fanatics. They were all trying to convince her that they had the Holy Grail, a mint condition 45 from Elvis's Sun sessions or something like that.

But yet, she felt a twinge of pity for this guy. He seemed so awkward and out of place. A hippie, that's what he looked like, she decided. He had the look of somebody who belonged in 1967, and he was out of place on the cusp of the 1980s, when people were harder-edged and obsessed with money and style.

"Okay," she said, swinging the door wide. "But I need some coffee first. And I'm warning you, I only buy records that are in good condition. Most people who come here are disappointed when they find out what their record is really worth."

"Oh, I think you'll be happy," he said, brushing past her. "My mother worked in the recording industry, and she collected this stuff years ago. These records are worthwhile."

He was carrying a brown paper shopping bag, and he went over and placed it on the counter next to the cash register. "Here, take a look."

"Not before I have my coffee," Rosie said. "You want a cup?"

"No thank you," the young man said. "I never drink the stuff."

"Suit yourself," Rosie said. She went around behind the counter and started the coffee maker. She always made sure to fill it up before she went to bed the night before, because she needed her coffee first thing in the morning, and she didn't want to waste time measuring out the coffee.

Within minutes there was the smell of Maxwell House coffee filling the air, and Rosie got a mug for herself from the collection on a shelf under the counter. She poured herself a cup while the young man waited impatiently, his eyes darting around the store, and when she had put in her cream and sugar and taken a healing sip of it, she came back over to the man and his paper bag.

"Okay," he said, reaching into the bag and pulling out a 45 in a sleeve. "Here's the first one. "The Criterions. 1959. 'I Remain Truly Yours'. This was their only hit."

Rosie looked at it, and saw that it was in good condition, looking like it had been played rarely. She put it on the turntable, turned on the record player, and placed the needle on it carefully.

The sounds of the song filled the store, and Rosie thrilled to the teenaged harmonies once again. It was a song about pledging undying love -- what else was there in the 1950s? -- and she marveled once again at the amazing harmonies these teenagers could produce.

When it was over, the young man said, "Well? What do you think?"

"It's somewhat rare," she said. "I don't have this particular record, but I have several others by this group. I can give you a few bucks for it, but this isn't a gold mine."

"Okay," he said. "Maybe you're right. But I have others. Look at this."

He pulled out a red vinyl 45 with a yellow label that said, "Unchained Melody" and the group was listed as "Vito and the Salutations". Rosie knew these guys had the unfortunate fate of releasing this song one week before The Beatles appeared on the Ed Sullivan show and wiped doo-wop off the pop charts forever. The record company had quickly destroyed thousands of copies of the single, and there were only a few dozen copies known to be still around.

"My God, where did your mother get this?" Rosie said. "I've never seen one."

"I told you, my mom worked in the record industry in New York," he said. "She was a secretary to Lew Schaefer, one of the most successful managers in the business back then. He didn't pay her a living wage, but he gave her lots of free records, cases and cases of them. My mom brought them all home and stored them in our attic. She always said they would be valuable some day."

"Your mom was a pretty smart cookie," Rosie said. "They are valuable, for sure. How much do you want for them?"

The young man looked at her with trusting eyes. "Whatever you want to pay for them," he said.

Rosie had just taken a big sip of her coffee, but she almost spit it out. "What do you mean?" she said. "Don't you have a price you're looking for?"

"No I don't," he said. "I'm just looking for whatever's fair. I don't care about the money. I don't even believe in money. I'm just looking to sell my mom's stuff and move to California. My lady and I want to move to a commune out there. We're not into material things, man. I guess you could say we're hippies. I don't like much about the life on the East Coast. I don't like all that disco music on the radio, I don't like how everybody is so obsessed with making money, and I don't like this guy Reagan who's just been elected President. I'm looking for a simpler life, one closer to the land. I'm just going to pack my things in my VW Beetle and move west with my girlfriend."

"Well, that's an interesting plan," Rosie said. "I bet you're going to find that you need more money than you think, though. Money has an annoying way of becoming necessary."

"That's why I'm here," the boy said. "I thought you'd buy some of my mom's records."

"Do you have more records like this?" Rosie said.

"I told you, there's a whole attic full of them," the boy said. "Do you want to come and look at them? I'll sell them all to you, for whatever price you name."

Rosie couldn't believe her luck. If the boy had a whole attic full of forgotten treasures like this one, it would mean a lot of money for her and the Dittybopper.

"Sure," she said. "I'd be interested in that. When do you want me to come?"

"No time like the present," the boy said. "I have my VW Beetle parked outside. Can you come now?"

Rosie thought it over for a second. The kid looked sincere, and although he was definitely a leftover hippie type, he seemed harmless. She had a soft spot for kids like that, who could just kick over the traces of their life and go off on their journeys of discovery. He reminded her of herself twenty years ago.

"Okay," she said. "Why not? Where do you live?"

"New Hope," the boy said.

CHAPTER TWO

Rosie put a sign in the window that the shop was closed for the day, and she got in her sensible blue Chevy Nova and followed the boy up Roosevelt Boulevard to New Hope. She liked the kid, but she was past the point of traveling in a beat up VW Beetle painted with rainbows and peace signs, mostly because she was too old to hitch hike if the little bug broke down.

Fall had come late this year, and even though it was the first week in November the trees were still laden with leaves, painted in riotous colors, and the sky was a deep turquoise color. They drove up the straight black ribbon of the Roosevelt Boulevard, past the neat little brick row houses and the ornate churches and synagogues built by immigrant families in the 1940s and 50s, and then as they got further north they drove past the Nabisco plant, smelling of chocolate chip cookies, which made Rosie feel happy and optimistic. There were other large plants and factories, and then farmland opening out as they went further north.

Rosie had been living in Northeast Philadelphia for two years now, running Dittybopper's record shop and acting as an office manager for his booming oldies' business. He was out almost every night of the week hosting oldies nights, playing the same records that he had ridden to fame twenty years before. He had a radio show again, and had opened a bar/restaurant in Philadelphia where he booked doo-wop acts and had his assistants spin records just like the old days.

Rosie had some money for the first time in her life, and even though Ditty paid her in cash and she wasn't entirely sure where it was coming from, she felt secure enough to buy some nice clothes, and a fancy car, and to get her hair and nails done once a week. She also sent money to her son Pete, now married to his African American girlfriend Betty, as a way of making up for the years when she was away during his childhood.

But she was still not satisfied with her life. There was something missing, just like there always had been. Oh, she had a decent romantic life -- she still had a thing for Bobby Juliano, who was reviving his career that had been aborted in the 1960s, and who was still handsome and youthful in his way. She knew that there was no future in it, though -- Bobby was just a neighborhood kid from South Philly, a simple boy who didn't ask for much from life.

And there was always Ditty, who amused her with his fast-talking and his street smarts, and who always kept things lively. It was like dating a whirlwind, though, and she sometimes found it exhausting. Not only that, there was a sadness about Ditty, because no matter how big he talked, no matter how much he strutted and preened, there was an air about him of someone whose time had passed. Rosie knew the music industry was a young person's business, and Ditty was in his 50s now -- he was too old to make it on the national stage. His moment, that one special, magical time in the early 1960s, had passed, he had missed the brass ring, and now the best he could do was to be a local celebrity, the kind of guy who was eventually going to be reduced to DJing weddings and retirement parties ten years from now.

There had been no one since James Charlesworth who had touched her deeply, and that had all happened so long ago. Her son from that union, Pete, was 33 years old, for God's sake. She hadn't seen Charlesworth since she left him in Ireland 10 years ago, and even though he had written her several letters since then, always wanting to come back in her life, she had never answered them.

14

Now the boy in the VW had turned off the Roosevelt Boulevard on to Woodhaven Road, and before long they were winding through the leafy lanes and winding roads of Bucks County. Rosie had rarely been in this part of Philadelphia. She remembered as a little girl her father had taken her to a house on the banks of the Delaware River, some mansion that looked like a castle, and she had been served parfaits by a waiter in tails. It was like a fairytale, and she almost expected to see a handsome prince ride up on his magnificent white horse and get off and kiss her hand.

But that was long ago, in another life, it seemed. It was so amazing to think where her life had led her since then, all the byways and alleys and ups and downs. But was she satisfied? No, not at all. There was still an itch for something else, although she didn't know what that was.

Before long the boy had turned onto the quaint main street of New Hope, with its shops and bookstores and vintage clothing stores, and restaurants with whimsical names, and the smell of marijuana in the air. The boy drove down Main Street and made a series of turns onto side streets until they came to a leafy lane with large gabled Victorian houses that could have been right out of the early 1900s. He pulled in the driveway of a particularly ramshackle one, and cut the motor off. Rosie pulled in behind him, and when she got out, he was standing there beaming.

"Well, here it is," he said. "This is our family's house."

The house was like something out of a hippie's dream. It had flowers everywhere, cats prowling the overgrown garden and sitting on the big old-fashioned rocking chairs on the porch, window pots with flowers spilling out of them, and that was just the outside. Inside it had an antique grandfather clock, an ornate marble fireplace with a large smoky mirror hanging over it, Impressionist paintings from the 19th century New Hope school of landscape painting, framed photographs from the early 1900s, brass fixtures in the kitchen, a checkerboard tiled floor, and everywhere there were vintage movie posters, psychedelic lights, books piled on every available flat surface, and a collection of old Victrola record players.

"This is quite a place," Rosie said. "Did you grow up here?"

"Yeah," the boy said. "My mom was born in this house. Lived here all her life."

"But I thought you said she worked in New York?"

"Sure. She commuted on the train. Schaefer had an apartment for her to stay in when she had too much work to do, which happened a lot. She stayed there usually three nights a week. My grandmother took care of me, she lived here too."

"You want some tea?" the boy said. "Some weed, maybe?"

"Uh, no thanks," Rosie said. "Well, no weed, thank you. I prefer to have a clear head when I'm working. I'll take a cup of tea, though."

"Sure," the boy said. He led Rosie into the kitchen and put a kettle of water on the stove. "By the way, I never told you my name. It's Kevin. I like to be called Embryo, though. You know, 'cause I feel like I'm just developing now, and I'll be born into another consciousness at some point."

"Embryo," Rosie said. "That's an interesting name."

"Yeah," the boy said. "You can call me Em. That's what my friends call me."

They chatted at the kitchen table and Em told her about his mother. "She was a character," he said. "She liked to collect things, as you can see. She thought it was important to hold on to interesting things. She called them "Lovely Bits". She didn't care for modern society much, just like me. She didn't want to move to California, though. She was happy here."

When the water boiled Em got up and poured it into a mug with a rainbow pattern on it, then dunked a tea bag in it and brought it over to Rosie. It had a sweet, peppermint smell that was bracing.

"Can we see the records now?" she asked.

"Oh, sure," Em said. "They're upstairs in the attic. I'll show you." He led the way up two flights of ancient wooden stairs, then up another six steps and through a panel in the ceiling to a large attic room. It smelled of old newspapers and cedar shavings, and Rosie saw it was crammed full of boxes of records.

"Wow," she said, giving an involuntary whistle. "I think you have more records here than I have back in the store. Your mother certainly collected a lot of vinyl. Is this all vocal groups from the Fifties?"

"No," Em said. "She liked all kinds of music. There are opera records here, Broadway show tunes, hillbilly music, folk music, big bands -- everything you can think of. I just mentioned the oldies stuff because I thought that's what you were interested in."

"I'm like your mother," Rosie said. "I like all kinds of music. I'm wrapped up in the oldies now, but that's not the only thing I listen to. All music speaks to my soul."

"That's a heavy idea, man," Em said. "I can dig that. Listen, why don't you sit in that big easy chair over there, and I'll bring some boxes over." He pointed to an overstuffed pink armchair with a floral pattern straight out of the 1920s. Rosie went over and sat in it, and Em started to bring her boxes of the records.

Rosie could not believe her eyes when she started looking through them. There were 45s from hundreds of early doo-wop groups, some of them still in their original cellophane covers, and many looking like they had never been put on a turntable. There were groups so rare she'd only heard about them, but had never heard the sound of their voices. It wasn't just big city groups, either, teens from New York or Philly or Baltimore. There were whole boxes of gospel records from the Deep South, blues artists, and other "race records", which was the euphemism used for black singers.

By way of explanation, Em said, "My mom's boss had a piece of a whole bunch of distribution companies, all over the country. He was involved in every part of the recording industry, and he even had a share in some radio stations. Some of it was pretty shady stuff, but the result was there were always boxes of records in the office, and like I said before, he let Mom take whatever samples she wanted. It was a way of making up for the fact that he didn't pay her very much. She worked for him all those years because she loved music, not because she was getting rich."

"Well, her loss is your gain," Rosie said. "Because, I have to be honest with you, some of this stuff is valuable."

"Whatever you say," Em said. "I trust you."

18

"You shouldn't trust so easily," Rosie said, her maternal instinct coming out. "Really, Em. I could cheat you."

"No, I trust you," he said. "I can tell. You have an honest face."

Rosie smiled and shook her head at the naiveté of youth. Was I ever that young? she thought. I guess I was. And I was just as innocent as him. Just as ready to take a fall when the world sucker punched me.

"Look," she said. "I'm just trying to be honest with you. You can't go around trusting every person you meet. I could be cheating you."

He spread his arms wide. "I don't believe that. You're an honest person, I can tell. I'll take whatever you think is fair for these records."

Rosie shook her head. "Okay. I promise I won't take advantage. I'll need time to look at these records and give you a quote. Do you have a yellow legal pad and a pen? I need to make some notes."

"Sure," he said. "I'll go downstairs and get you something." He turned to go, then stopped and turned around. "You know, I believe in past lives. And I felt when I saw you that we knew each other in a past life. That's why I trust you."

"Well, maybe so," Rosie said. "But I hope you realize that you should be planning for the future in this life, not worrying about past ones."

Listen to me, she thought. I never worried about the future myself, especially not at this kid's age.

Maybe I should start, she thought, looking at the treasure spread around her.

CHAPTER THREE

"It's a crime what the British are doing in Ireland," Larry Flynn said, ordering another round of beers. "They've never forgiven us for winning our freedom in the South, and they're trying to drive all the Catholics out of the North. Bloody bastards." He drained his beer in one gulp and wiped his mouth with the back of his hand.

Pete felt the bile rise in him again, and his fists clenched under the table as his buddies ranted on about Ireland. He'd never been to Ireland, but he knew his great-grandparents had come from there, and in recent years he'd been more and more transfixed by The Troubles, the war between the Catholics and Protestants in Northern Ireland, with the British Army in the middle of it. He came to O'Toole's Irish bar in Southwest Philadelphia almost every night, and he'd watch the news about the latest atrocity and rant with his friends, or sing belligerent Irish songs.

His wife Betty was never with him. She wasn't happy when he went to O'Toole's, but she went along with it reluctantly when he told her he needed the nights out. "This is the only thing that helps with these nightmares I get, and the panic attacks," he said. The truth was, it wasn't the camaraderie of the bar but the alcohol that kept the Beast at bay, although he didn't want to admit that.

He didn't like to think that he had a drinking problem, but in his sober moments he wondered about the path he was headed on.

It had all started after he married Betty two years ago. Actually, to be accurate, it was after Betty got pregnant and their daughter Rosalie was born. Something about being a father scared him so much that he couldn't sleep at night. Holding that helpless baby in his arms brought back all the terrors of Vietnam, made him feel like he was nothing but a rough, violent, brutal man in comparison to the purity and innocence of his daughter.

It was supposed to be a happy time. He'd survived the war, he was back home, he'd married a beautiful black woman named Betty Taylor, he had a baby daughter, and even a row house in the city. His mother Rosie was home from her crazy footloose lifestyle in the 1960s and 70s, and they were repairing their damaged relationship.

But still he got the fear. It came on him sometimes without warning, triggered by a sudden car backfiring, or a plane overhead, or the squeal of air brakes on a city bus. Any sudden noise could do it, and in an instant he would be in a crouch, looking for his gun, scanning the area for hostile movement, ready to lash out at anything that seemed suspicious.

But the fear was only part of the problem. There were other times when a black depression would come on him, and it was like he was a zombie, the living dead, walking and talking and doing his job, but unable to feel anything.

The way he dealt with that, besides drinking, was by gambling. He found that betting money helped him to forget his pain. It gave him a rush when he won, and when he lost, well, he just shrugged it off. Losing a few dollars wasn't going to hurt him. He'd seen men lose their lives in battle; losing a day's pay was nothing compared to that.

He liked to wager on card games, pool, even darts, at O'Toole's. He was terrible at cards, mediocre at pool, and he was only good at darts if he had one beer in him; anything more, and it would throw off his shot.

He lost small amounts of money for a while, but it was manageable until he started going to the casinos in Atlantic City with his buddies. He started to lose bigger sums, and it wasn't long before he was borrowing money from Larry Flynn and the other guys. Things became more serious then; he realized he was getting in over his head, but he kept trying to hit a winning streak that would make it all turn out right.

Betty didn't know how deeply he was in debt, but she knew he was a ball of nerves and she wanted him to get help. He didn't see what good it would do to talk to a psychiatrist. This was just something he had to get through, that was all.

Betty was not happy staying home with Rosalie, and Pete knew that contributed to the problem. She had a law degree and wanted to use it, but Pete convinced her that Rosalie needed a mother home with her, that he didn't want any child of his to go through the loneliness he felt when his mother left him to fly off to London and be a part of the Swinging Sixties.

So they were living on one income, the money he made from the auto body shop, and it wasn't enough, the wages he made for banging out dents in cars. He needed more, but he didn't want to go back to school to get a degree, and he didn't want to become a cop, like so many of the guys in his neighborhood had done. He'd had enough of guns and their madness for one life.

He was a stubborn man, Pete Morley. He didn't listen to anybody. The neighborhood he lived in was pure working class white, and there were no blacks living within five miles of it. All except for his wife, Betty. He didn't give a hoot about what anybody thought, and if any of his buddies so much as mentioned Betty's skin color in a derogatory way, Pete wouldn't hesitate to rearrange the guy's face. He'd lost a few friends because of that, but in time the people in the neighborhood learned to treat Betty with respect and even goodwill.

Betty always held her head high when she walked, and she talked to everyone like she was their equal, no matter who they were. She had no fear, and she just acted as if the world was a better place than it really was. However, there were times when she wondered why Pete had to pick Southwest Philly to live in.

"I'm just comfortable here, that's all," he said.

Comfortable with guys like Larry Flynn, tough characters who, as Betty said, "have more street smarts than common sense." She didn't like Larry, and resented the time Pete spent with him. Larry was always coming up with some plan that she thought could get Pete into trouble.

Like tonight. The other guys left Pete and Larry alone while they went off to play a game of pool in the back room, and Larry turned to Pete.

"You know," he said, lowering his voice. "I know some people who are helping our brothers out in the old country."

"Helping?" Pete said. "How are they helping?"

"They're providing them with what they need most -- guns, bombs, ammunition. It's a war over there, Pete, and the Brits and Protestants won't quit until we drive them out of our ancestral land. But it's like any other war -- the winners will be the ones with the most firepower."

"That's the way it usually works," Pete said. "Although it wasn't true in Nam. We had lots more firepower than the Vietnamese, but they drove us out."

"Ah, there was too much politics, too much dirty dealing, in that war," Flynn said. "This one is going to be won with the firepower, and the guts of the people fighting. But, Pete," he said, lowering his voice and leaning closer, "we have to do our part to help them."

"What do you mean?" Pete said.

"They don't have the resources over there to fight the British army, boy. We need to provide it to them. There are people over here who are doing their part to help out. But it's a dirty business, and care must be taken. Secrecy must be maintained. It's hard to find people who can fit the bill. I think you could be someone who could help us, Pete."

"How do you mean?"

"By helping us to transport the needed supplies to them."

"You mean take guns to them?" Pete was dumbstruck.

"Lower your voice," Larry said, leaning closer. "You can't trust anyone when it comes to this business, and there could be someone listening who shouldn't hear this. Yes, we're giving them the firepower they need. There are a lot of people involved, both here and over there. What we need on this end are people who can transport the stuff to a sort of way station where it will be taken overseas to our comrades. It's a risky business, but you'll have the satisfaction of knowing you're helping your brothers in arms."

"I don't know," Pete said. "That has to be illegal, right? I don't know if that's something I should be getting mixed up in. Besides, I had enough of guns during Nam. I don't care if I never see one of those things again. They don't solve anything."

"That's a noble sentiment," Larry said, taking a sip of his beer, "but a misguided one. There are times when the only negotiation worth its salt is with the barrel of a gun. Gun power is what's needed over there, Pete, and they're desperate for it on our side."

"I don't like it," Pete said, running a hand through his hair nervously. "Where do you get this stuff? You can't just go in a store and buy a truckload of AK-47s."

"It's not for you to worry about," Flynn said. "There are people involved in this business at many levels. Some of them are people you don't want to know too well, if you know what I mean. It's better not to ask too many questions. All you need to do is drive a truck from here to Boston several times a month. You don't ask questions, and you won't know anything that can hurt you."

Pete shrugged. "Sorry, I don't think I want to get mixed up in it. I support the Irish Catholics, but this--"

"There's money in it," Flynn said. "And that's something you could use, my friend."

"I know I owe you money," Pete said, picking up on Flynn's meaning. "I'll pay you and the other guys back, don't worry."

"Oh, I know you will," Larry said, cracking his knuckles. "I'm a reasonable man, Pete. It's not me you have to worry about, no not me. It's the other boys. Some of them are getting a bit agitated about the amount of money you owe them. They've been talking about," he paused, and cracked his knuckles again, very loudly, "oh, I don't know, finding ways to convince you. They're not very patient people, you see. They're prone to a certain rashness where money is concerned."

"Look, if I had it I'd pay them," Pete said. "I just don't have it right now. There's no way for me to--"

"To get the money?" Larry said. "But that's what I'm talking to you about. You can make a nice tidy sum by just doing a few jobs for us. It's easy work, and you'll earn enough to pay back your debts. It's not a bad deal, Pete. I'd think about it if I were you."

Pete took a drink of his beer. "How much money?" he said.

"A thousand dollars a shipment," Larry said. "Paid in cash by my associates in Boston. Like I said, it would be no more than two trips a month. But that's a nice boost to your wallet, for a couple of ten hour round trips a month."

Pete thought it over. Betty had been complaining a lot lately about needing more money for various bills that they had. It would be nice to have some extra cash, maybe buy some new dresses for her and Rosalie. He loved it when she got all decked out and they went out on the town, but it hadn't happened in so long.

"When were you thinking I'd do this?" Pete said. "I have a day job, you know. I can't do it during the week. Weekends are the only time I'm free."

Flynn smiled and slapped his hand on Pete's shoulder. "Then that's when we'll do it. Meet me here on Friday night, and we'll do the first shipment this weekend."

27

CHAPTER FOUR

Rosie needed a break from the detail work of examining and classifying each record in the attic, and at one in the afternoon she told Em she wanted to walk around the town of New Hope for an hour.

"Sure," he said. "That's a fine idea, man. I can show you a good natural foods restaurant where they make dandelion wine and tofu pancakes. I know the owner, and he grows his own weed."

"Thanks," Rosie said, "but I think I'll just explore the town myself. It looks like an interesting place. I'll be back in an hour."

She knew that Em's house was just a couple of blocks off the main street of the town, and since it was an unseasonably balmy day, she decided to walk. Within minutes she was at the main street, and she wandered happily among the head shops and vintage clothing and antique stores, the smell of incense mixing with hamburgers from the restaurants she passed.

There was one quaint little alley off the main street, and when she went down it she passed a coffee shop, a little cafe, and then a beautiful old Victorian house with faded blue shutters and a porch. The place looked like it had been a hotel in better days. It was dilapidated now, with broken windows and loose floorboards on the porch, and a general air of decay about it. There was a man standing on the porch peering through a greasy window, and he turned to look at her as she stood in front of the house looking it over.

"It's an eyesore, isn't it?" he said.

"I don't think I'd call it that," she said. "It's beautiful. It just needs some work, that's all."

28

"Work?" he snorted. "It's falling apart. It would take a lot of work to fix this place up. They ought to just tear it down."

"You don't have much feeling for history," Rosie said.

"Sure I do," he said. "I just don't like to put the past on a pedestal. If it's standing in the way of progress, mow it down. I look at things and I see the future, not the past."

He had longish platinum colored hair that swept over his ears like corn silk, and the most penetrating blue eyes Rosie had ever seen. He was lean and wiry, and had a wry smile at the corners of his mouth. He looked cerebral but very physical at the same time. He was wearing a brown bomber jacket and jeans, but his body gave off the aura of physicality, like he was a panther at rest, coiled muscles always ready to spring.

Rosie laughed. "Well, that's not an attitude I would expect to hear in this quaint little town. Every other shop seems to be selling old clothing or antiques. And there's a distinct aroma of marijuana around here. Seems a lot of people are stuck in the 1960s. I think it's charming, though."

"Charming?" the man said. "Yeah, I guess you could call it that. I'm not a big fan of charming, though. There's too much happening in the world today, too many big things coming, to be stuck in charming mode."

"You must feel out of place around here," Rosie said, laughing again.

"Sure do," he said. He came over and held out his hand. "Sorry, about my manners. My name's Caldwell. Jack Caldwell. Nice to meet you."

29

Rosie shook his hand, and it felt like the hand of a carpenter or bricklayer. His fingers were calloused and his grip was strong.

"My name's Rose Morley," she said. "Everybody calls me Rosie. Nice to meet you. What is this place, by the way? Do you know the history of it? Unless history is too boring a subject for you."

"No, I like history," he said. "I just don't like giving it more importance than it should have. This place? It's the old River Inn. It was built during the time when the canal was a major thoroughfare around here. You've heard of the Delaware River canal? For a hundred years boats would bring coal from Easton through here, on their way to Bristol to be loaded on to ships. The boatmen used to stay at this hotel, along with traders and visitors from all over the East Coast. It was a grand place back in its day. That was long ago, though. The canal hasn't been a functioning waterway for 25 years. The last owners of this place couldn't keep up with it, and it deteriorated. They went bankrupt five years ago, and the place has been vacant ever since."

"It's a shame," Rosie said. "A place with this much history. There are probably ghosts inside, reliving scenes from the glory days."

Jack smiled, and the creases at the side of his brilliant blue eyes showed. "Ghosts? I don't know if I believe in them, but if they exist, sure, there are probably a few associated with this old place. I've heard stories about things happening here, a murder or two in the last hundred years, which would probably mean there are ghosts hanging around."

"I love places like this," Rosie said. "You know, I've always wanted to open a bar and restaurant in a place like this. A place with character. This would be perfect."

"Well, why don't you do it?" Jack said. "What's holding you back?"

"Oh, I don't know," she said. "It's probably another of my foolish ideas. I tend to jump into things without thinking enough. It's not a very practical thing to do, is it?"

"The hell with practical," Jack said. "That kind of thinking gets in the way of creativity. Hey, would you like to get lunch? I was just thinking of grabbing a bite to eat, and I know a good restaurant nearby that serves decent food."

Rosie knew she should get back to cataloging the records, but she couldn't resist this man's smile and twinkling eyes.

"Sure," she said. "I have some business near here, but I can take a short break. Lead the way."

Jack Caldwell took her down the street and around the corner to a little cafe on the banks of the Delaware River, and they sat outside and watched scullers rowing on the water in the gorgeous late fall day.

They ordered sandwiches and beers, and Rosie asked Jack about his life. "So, what do you do?" she said.

"I'm a futurist," he said.

"What in the hell is that?" she said, laughing.

"I think about the future. I prognosticate. I dream up scenarios about what the world will be like in 20, 30, 50 years."

"You do that for a job?"

"Oh, I pay the bills in lots of creative ways. But, yes, I am often paid for my ability to look into the future. Companies, think tanks, various organizations use me for strategic planning."

Rosie took a sip of her beer, and smiled. "Are you psychic?"

He laughed. "No, I don't really believe in psychic abilities. Although people have accused me of being a psychic from time to time, when my predictions come true."

"Okay," Rosie challenged. "Give me an example of a prediction that came true."

Jack smiled again, and the corners of his eyes creased. "Okay, I'll give you one. I predicted the psychedelic era almost ten years before it happened. I wrote a report on it when I had a government job back in 1959, and I still have the report in a file cabinet at home. I predicted the whole thing -- the rise of LSD use, the hippie culture, all of it."

"You did, huh?" Rosie said. "That's pretty impressive. I remember 1959, and there was no inkling of anything like what was going to happen in the 1960s that year. Girls were still wearing girdles and beehive hairdos and taking classes in etiquette. Nobody knew what was coming. How did you know?"

"It wasn't rocket science. I just paid attention. I was living in San Francisco and working for. . . well, let's just say I worked for a government agency that was in the business of collecting information on people. I knew about the experiments that were going on at the time, where they were giving mental patients doses of this strange new drug that gave them hallucinations, euphoria, radical new insights. I took a few doses myself, under laboratory conditions. I knew this stuff was powerful, and it was going to change people's heads."

"So, you were an early hippie?"

"No, like I said, it was part of my job to find out about things like this. My agency was trying to find ways to use drugs like LSD in various ways, maybe as a truth serum. There was an ulterior motive, I guess you'd say. But once I took some of it, I realized there was no way they were going to be able to keep a lid on this stuff. It was too powerful. Do you know, there were people in the movie industry, big stars like Cary Grant, who were taking it back then? They'd do it in laboratories, with a bunch of doctors in white coats monitoring them, but still, they were on LSD trips."

The waitress brought them their orders, and she was dressed in a flowered peasant dress and had her long hair braided. She was wearing beads and sandals, too. When she left, Rosie pointed to her and said: "So, you predicted that a whole generation would dress like that?"

He took a bite of his chicken sandwich and laughed. "I think I underestimated it a bit. I thought psychedelic culture would be confined to a small niche, sort of like the beatniks. Small pockets of hippies in places like San Francisco and New York. I didn't realize it would be such a huge cultural phenomenon. It taught me a lesson: I should always go with the bigger, more radical predictions. Life is stranger than we think, and change is faster than we expect."

"So what are you predicting now?"

33

He took another bite and his eyes seemed to glow brighter blue. "Oh, some amazing things. Absolutely stunning. The next twenty or thirty years are going to be some of the most creative, path breaking, radical ones in history. It's going to be a wild ride, so hold on to your hat."

Rosie snorted. "That's hard to believe. The last century has been pretty earth shattering, if you ask me. I mean, besides rock 'n roll, hippies, the Vietnam war, the Kennedy assassination, the Moon landing, the Middle East wars, and about fifty other things from recent times, there's two World Wars, a Depression, the Holocaust, famines, and a lot of other things that are pretty world changing."

He laughed again. "You're right, the Twentieth Century has been a real crazy one. But I'm telling you, things are going to start really heating up now."

"Okay, I'll bite. What's going to happen?"

"Technology. Technology is going to change all of our lives in ways we can't imagine. Have you ever worked with a computer?"

Rosie wrinkled her nose. "Ugh. No. All I know is that every time there's a problem with my bank account, or my phone bill, the companies blame it on the computers. 'Our computers are down,' they say. It's an all-purpose excuse for every delay or problem."

Jack laughed. "I know, but that's because the computers today are big clunky things that are just too weak and slow to do what companies want them to do. And they're run by people who have no vision, no idea of what they're capable of. No, there's a revolution coming in the computer field, and you won't believe what's going to happen."

"Oh, you've seen the future of computing, then?"

"Yes. I told you I lived in California, and that's where it's really taking off. I live here now, but I go back to the West Coast a lot, because that's where the action is, and I like to stay up on what's happening. There are people out there, some of them only teenagers, who are building computers in their garages, and they're doing some amazing things. There's a guy named Steve Jobs who I stay in touch with, and I promise you that fellow is going to go down in history as a world changer."

"Kids?" Rosie said. "You're telling me that teenagers are going to be behind the next big thing in history? That's hard to believe."

"It's true. These kids are making computers that are so useful they'll be in everyone's home in five years."

Rosie had just taken a sip of water, and she almost spit it out. "That's crazy. It will never happen. Nobody will want those big, stupid machines in their houses."

"They won't be big, and they won't be stupid, I promise you," he said. "They're going to get smaller all the time, yet faster and more powerful. It's coming, as sure as I'm sitting here. But that's only the start of it. There will come a time when we're all connected on a huge computer network, a worldwide network that transmits human knowledge at the speed of thought. Imagine -- there will be so much information, so much knowledge speeding around that our collective intelligence will increase exponentially. We'll be smarter than ever before, healthier, living longer -- it will be a paradise."

"I don't know," Rosie said. "It sounds like science fiction to me."

He laughed. "The most far out science fiction writers haven't even dreamed of this. Well, actually, there is one -- a guy named William Gibson. I met him at a science fiction writer's conference in Canada recently. He's a visionary, I think, and he's got a great sense of where we're headed. I'm going to keep my eye on him. It's people like him and Steve Jobs who are going to have the ideas that will change the world. Change is coming, Rosie, and we're all going to benefit from it.

"But enough about me," he said, smiling. "What do you do?"

"I'm in the record business," she said. "Oldies, to be exact."

He laughed out loud. "Oldies? You mean that tired old music, the doo-wop stuff from the Fifties? Wow, you're really living in the past."

CHAPTER FIVE

"That's a cheeky comment," Rosie said. "You don't even know me. Besides, there's nothing wrong with the past, mister. It's comforting for a lot of people to hear the music they danced to in high school. Those are the best years of their lives, for some people. We never forget the music from those days."

He grinned, and the edges of his eyes crinkled in an appealing way. "High school? The best years of your life? Are you kidding me? If high school was the best time of my life, I'd shoot myself. I was a skinny, clumsy kid with a face full of acne in high school. I wouldn't go back to those years if you paid me a million dollars."

"Some people have happy memories from that time," Rosie said. "It's comforting for them to look back. It was a simpler time, there was less anxiety to it."

"My God, no, that's wrong," he said, sitting on the edge of his chair and waving his hands with emotion. "You're romanticizing it. It was never that way. Life is so rich, so full of new, exciting things. You can't get stuck in the past."

"I'm not stuck in the past!"

"You're making a career out of it," he said. "You're part of this oldies boom on the radio. I bet you play those moldy old records at dances for people who are trying to recapture their youth."

Rosie was miffed at him again. "I work for Howie Moss, the Dittybopper. He's a DJ who has his own oldies show on the radio, and yes, he does put on dances several times a week. It's a growing business, let me tell you. It's getting more popular all the time. People like that music."

He smirked. "I'm sure they do. There are lots of people who don't want to face the present, or the future. They'd rather live in the past. So, tell me, what are you doing in New Hope today? I don't see anybody around here dressed like the guys from Sha Na Na, with those shiny gold jackets and greased back hair."

"I am an expert on oldies records," she said. "I'm here to appraise somebody's record collection, because we buy old records whenever we can."

He shook his head wryly. "You really are in this with both feet, aren't you? God, you even buy and sell these old vinyl platters."

"It's a good investment," she said, defensively. "These records have been appreciating in value. People make money off them, I'll have you know."

"I'll tell you a good investment," Jack said, leaning closer. "My friends in California tell me that in about a month that guy Steve Jobs I told you about and his partners are going to take their company, Apple Computer, public. You buy shares in that company, and you'll make a million dollars a lot faster than you will by selling old records. The smart people are the ones who are focused on the future, not the past."

Rosie had just taken a sip of beer, but she put the glass down on the table with a clatter. "You have a lot of nerve, buddy. I don't like your insinuation that I'm not smart, just because of the business I'm in. I don't care how much you know about the future, or how smart you think you are, I'm happy doing what I do. I'm in the business of nostalgia, sure, but it's something pleasant for people, it gives them relief from their dreary adult lives. For a moment or two they can relive the happy days of their youth. It's better than all this pie in the sky stuff you do, cheerleading for some rosy future that will never come true."

She got up, fished a twenty-dollar bill out of her purse, and slapped it on the table. "Here," she said. "This should be enough to pay for our meal. That's money I made from trading in nostalgia, but it's just as good for paying for a beer and a sandwich as whatever you make from your futuristic twaddle. Now if you'll excuse me, I have to go back and finish cataloguing some musty old records."

She walked off, leaving Jack Caldwell with a bemused expression on his handsome face.

Rosie stormed off in the direction of Em's house, but she quickly got lost. She found she didn't remember exactly how to get there, and she didn't even know the name of his street. She so was furious at this smug man, Jack Caldwell, for belittling her work that she couldn't even focus on finding the way home. She walked down a side street and found herself in front of a small shop that had a sign that said, "Psychic -- ESP -- Learn Your Future".

I'll just go in there and ask for directions, she thought. People in this town must know Em, if his family has lived here for his whole life, like he told me.

She went in the door and immediately smelled incense burning. There was some heady, exotic music playing, something with a sitar and tabla drums, probably Ravi Shankar. There were a few chairs scattered around, and a comfortable looking maroon couch, and the decor was a combination of psychedelic, gypsy, and space alien. A plump, middle-aged woman came through a beaded curtain in the back and said, "Welcome!"

She was dressed in a paisley print long flowing dress, with a red bandana around her head, dangling silver earrings, and rings on every finger. She had heavy makeup, especially around her eyes. Rosie couldn't tell if she was really some exotic gypsy woman or just a housewife playing a part.

"Are you here to get your fortune told?" the woman said.

"Actually, I'm just lost," Rosie said. "I was looking for directions."

"You came to the right place," the woman said, holding out her hand. "I am Ruth. I specialize in helping lost people. We all have a purpose, my dear, and I can help you find yours. Why don't you sit down and we'll get started."

"No," Rosie said. "I don't mean I'm lost in my life. I'm just lost in this town. I need to find a big Victorian house on a tree-lined street. It's got blue shutters. There's a young man who lives there. . ."

Ruth laughed. "Do you know how many houses fit that description? But, seriously, you look like someone who could use a session with the crystal ball. Why don't you come and find out what Life has in store for you?"

"No, I need to get back," Rosie said. "I just need directions to the house."

Ruth would not be denied, however. "Tell you what. I'll help you find that house if you sit down and have a ten-minute session with me. I can give you a lot of direction in ten minutes. You look like someone who could use it."

Rosie laughed. She knew the woman was just trying to get a sale, but at least she did it with good humor. And she did always feel like she didn't have much of a plan in her life. Maybe this woman had a smattering of psychic ability, and it would be good to find out what she had to say.

"All right," she said. "I'm game. But I don't have a lot of time to spare."

The woman clapped her hands. "No problem! I can tell a lot in ten minutes. Come with me." She led Rosie to the back, through the beaded curtain to a small room down a corridor, and it was redolent of sweet-smelling incense burning in a copper brazier. The light was soft, from several candles burning on various small tables scattered around the room. There was a larger table in the middle, and two comfortable leather chairs on either side of it. On the table was a large crystal ball.

"Please, sit," Ruth said, pointing to one of the chairs.

Rosie sat down at one chair, and Ruth took the other. She immediately asked Rosie to put her hands on either side of the crystal ball. She closed her eyes, mumbled some kind of a prayer or incantation, and then opened them and stared fixedly at the ball.

"You have had an interesting past," she said.

Well, that's a pretty vague statement, Rosie thought. She was wary of saying too much, because she knew the frauds in this business often tried to get their clients to give away more information than they wanted to.

"I can see you have suffered a lot," the woman said. "You have had problems with men."

Rosie held back the urge to laugh. Every woman who came in here probably was having problems with men, so that wasn't big news either.

"You have a son."

That was closer to the mark, but again --

"He has a daughter, whose name is similar to yours."

Rosie sucked in her breath. This was getting closer to the truth. She struggled not to show any emotion, not to give anything away to this woman.

"Your son. . . he is married to a black woman."

Rosie's heart skipped a beat. How could this woman know that?

"He loves her very much, but he causes her anguish. I see the sadness in her eyes. He is getting mixed up in a bad business, and it will cause her pain. And you."

This was getting a bit too intense. "Hey, I thought people like you only gave good news," Rosie said. "It's not good business to scare the customers, is it?"

The woman looked at her for a second, appraising her, and said, "You are strong enough for it. Some people can't handle bad news, but you can."

Rosie sighed. "All right. What's this thing he's mixed up in. What's it all about?"

"Ireland," the woman said. "It has to do with Ireland. There are guns. Violence. He should get away from this situation, or he will get hurt."

Rosie shuddered. She knew that Pete had been getting more involved in the Irish Troubles; it was something he talked about all the time. She figured he was trying to find an identity, to connect with his roots, and that was why he'd developed this obsession with the Protestant-Catholic conflict in the north of Ireland. He seemed so angry about it, though -- his face would get red and the veins in his neck would pop out when he talked about it, and he used words like "retribution", "revenge", and "injustice".

Rosie shrugged her shoulders. "Okay, I get that. I'll see what I can do. What else? Shouldn't you be telling me about my love life?"

The woman smiled. "That is going fine. I see no problems there."

Rosie giggled. "Really? Well, that would be a considerable improvement over the status quo. Can you give me some details?"

"Oh, you've already met him. A handsome fellow he is, too. He will help you to throw off the past."

Rosie shivered. It sounded like this guy Jack Caldwell she just met. Could it be him? "What does he look like?" she said, giving Ruth a hard stare, like a detective grilling a suspect.

"Oh, he has a great head of white hair, and the bluest eyes this side of a beach on Bermuda. He's got a warm smile, and a sharp mind. And beautiful hands."

Rosie blushed. It was Jack. "But what do you mean, he'll help me throw off the past? I don't feel any burden from--"

"You are weighed down by it," she said. "You carry it with you everywhere, and your spirit is groaning under its weight. You can hardly move forward at all because of its burden."

"That's ridiculous," Rosie snapped. "I love the past. I make my living from it. It's not holding me back at all. I don't know what you mean."

Ruth smiled, but it was a penetrating smile. "You have been hurt, like we all have, but you carry it around with you. You can't move forward until you leave your hurt behind."

Rosie pushed her chair back with a squeak and stood up. "I've heard enough," she said. "How much do I owe you? I don't have time for this nonsense."

Ruth put her hand out and grabbed Rosie's wrist. "I know it is difficult to hear. But you are strong enough to hear it. Please sit down."

Rosie sat down reluctantly. "Really, I was under the impression that you were only going to give me some pabulum, that you were going to sugar coat everything and tell me I was going to win the lottery, then collect your fee and send me on my way. I wasn't expecting--"

"I know," Ruth said. "You weren't expecting anything that would upset you. But I deal in the truth, not fairy tales. The truth can empower you, however. Do you want to hear more?"

Rosie sighed, and straightened her shoulders. "Okay. I guess I can handle this."

Ruth looked at the crystal ball again. "You have a beautiful voice. I can hear it. You love to sing, but you don't do it anymore. You stopped singing."

Rosie blushed. "I don't get many opportunities these days. Singing was fun, but the music industry is fickle, and I'm in a different part of it now. My days of singing in front of an audience are over."

"Why?"

"I just told you, it's not something I do anymore. I had fun with it when I was younger, but you can't stand in front of a microphone and sing love songs when you're my age."

"Why not?"

"Because it looks silly, doesn't it? I'm too old for--"

"For what? Bringing some beauty into the world with your voice? For doing what you have loved since you were a little girl? For falling in love with music again? For falling in love with a man again?"

Rosie chuckled. "Boy, this is like going to a therapist. You missed your calling, lady. You should have gotten a degree in

Psychiatry. All you need is a couch for me to lay on, and this would be no different than--"

"Answer the question," Ruth said. "You're avoiding it."

"I told you, I'm too old for that."

"So, you've given up your dream?"

Rosie bristled. "I gave it a shot, but it didn't work out. I was too young to really be part of the big band era, but too old when doo-wop came along, and definitely too old when rock hit. The timing was all off. It's done, over with, and I can't do anything about it."

"You could still have it, if you want it," Ruth said. "It's all up to you."

CHAPTER SIX

September 1983

"Rosalie, let's go see the lions," Pete said. His tow-headed daughter Rosalie had her hand in his, and she had a huge grin on her face, because it was her favorite outing to go to the zoo on Sunday afternoons like this.

Pete was happy to be here with her. She was almost four years old, and she had a personality that was all fizz and sparkle. She woke up every morning ready to be happy, and the world never disappointed her. She had her mother Betty's caramel colored skin, but Pete's emerald green eyes and a shock of frizzy blondish hair. She was the joy of Pete's life, and she was the one bright spot right now in his world.

Things hadn't been going well with Rosalie's mother these days. Betty had been chafing at Pete's wish to have her be a stay-at-home mother. "I worked hard to get my law degree, Pete," she said often. "I want to use it. I love Rosalie, but I know lots of moms my age who work. There are a lot of good day care centers around the city."

"Yeah, and who's taking care of those kids?" Pete would say. "A bunch of strangers, who don't really care about the kids. It's a job to them, Betty, not something they love, and the kids know it. Believe me, a child needs its mother around."

Betty would roll her eyes and say, "Oh, here it comes again, how deprived you were because your mother ran off to England when you were a teenager. Well, first of all, I'm not your mother and I'm not going to leave my child like that. I'll be home every night to feed her dinner, listen to how her day went, and tuck her in. And you know I give her lots of hugs and kisses, Pete. I love her to death, but there's a part of me that needs to work. I need to be around smart people and do meaningful work."

And that was the part of the argument where Pete would say, "Oh, so I'm not smart enough for you, huh?" and things always went downhill from there.

It was getting worse all the time. And now, as if to add even more complications, Betty was pregnant again. She was just under three months pregnant, but it had been a hot summer and the heat made her morning sickness worse. She felt miserable most of the time, and the prospect of another baby wasn't cheering her up. Pete was happy to be a father again, although he still wasn't making enough money at the auto body shop, which is why he supplemented his income running his truckloads of "supplies" up to Boston and New York.

He hadn't told Betty all the details, but she was smart enough to figure a lot of it out by herself. She knew that Pete was running guns that were eventually going to find their way across the Atlantic to the IRA fighters in Northern Ireland. It was something she couldn't understand, why Pete would put himself in such danger for a country he'd never been to.

"You don't get it," he'd say. "My roots are there. My mother's family came from Ireland. Sure it was in Skibbereen, in the south of the country, but the fact is that all Irish people should be free of the British oppressors, and in the north they're not."

"You're just parroting that nonsense you hear from Larry Flynn and the other idiots you hang with it at that bar," Betty said. "They're weekend warriors, guys who've never done any fighting themselves, but they sit on their barstools and spout slogans and rhetoric."

"They're helping our people," Pete said, "and that's enough for me."

Usually at that point Pete would have to leave, or the argument would go on for hours. He still loved Betty, but there was a wedge between them now, and he didn't know how to get rid of it.

"Daddy, I don't want to go see the lions," Rosalie said, digging her heels in and pointing to the lion house. "It's scary in there. I can hear them roaring."

Betty had told Pete not to take Rosalie to the lion house when he left this morning. Betty was going to church with her mother and she planned to meet Pete and Rosalie at the zoo afterward. "Rosalie doesn't like the lion house, so don't take her there," Betty had said. "She doesn't like loud noises, and the sound echoes off the walls in that place. The lions will start roaring and she'll get scared."

"No problem, I won't take here there," Pete said, but he was lying. He was supposed to meet one of his contacts at the zoo, and the man had told Larry Flynn he'd meet Pete inside the lion house at one o'clock on Sunday. There was no way to get in touch with him to change the meeting plan, so Pete had to do it.

"It's okay," he told Rosalie. "The lions are in big, strong cages with iron bars. They can't get out."

"But I don't like the noise," she said. "They're too loud."

49

"I'll protect you," Pete said. He picked her up in his arms. "Daddy is very strong. I'm not afraid of those noisy lions."

Rosalie looked uncertain, and she bit her lip. Finally, she seemed to relax in Pete's strong arms. "Okay," she said. "If you say so. But don't put me down."

"I won't," he said. He walked into the lion house, which was a brick building built in the 1930s that had tile floors and walls, which amplified the sound of the lions when they roared. Pete had been there before and he knew the lions were usually sleeping or lying on the floor with bored expressions on their faces, unless it was feeding time.

Unfortunately, there was a large sign inside the door that said, "The lions are fed at 1 PM every day."

Pete realized it was close to feeding time. It was ten minutes to one, and the lions were pacing nervously back and forth, waiting for their food. Their muscles rippled under their smooth coats, and they walked with silent, padding footsteps in spite of their huge bulk.

"They're so big," Rosalie said, her eyes wide.

"They're just big cats, that's all," Pete said. "Really, they're no different than our cat Snowball at home. They're just a little bigger, that's all."

The lion house was filling up with spectators, because people liked to see the big cats feasting on the raw steaks they were fed. Pete scanned the room for his contact, and he saw a man wearing sunglasses and a green Philadelphia Eagles shirt over his jeans, sitting in the top row of the benches that lined the far wall. The man nodded when he saw Pete, and Pete started to climb up toward him.

"Where are we going?" Rosalie said.

"Oh, just to the top row of the benches," Pete said. "You don't want to be near the cages, do you?"

"No!" Rosalie said. "I want to be far away from those noisy lions."

"Don't worry, we will be," Pete said. He climbed up and sat next to the man in the sunglasses. Rosalie was fixated on the lions, and she hardly noticed when the man spoke to Pete.

"Did you hear what happened?" he said, his voice low. "A bunch of the lads broke out of the Maze prison. Thirty-eight of them, I think it was. Ah, it's a glorious day for us."

"Yes," Pete said. "I saw it on the news. It is a happy development, to be sure." He tended to have the hint of an Irish lilt to his voice when he was talking about Ireland, and this time was no different.

"They'll be after them, though," the man said. "Faith, their lives are in great danger."

"I know. I hope they have friends who will shelter them."

"There are many patriots in Ireland," the man whispered. "But not enough over here. Over here you have the lily-livered kind, that likes to sing the revolutionary songs at the bar, and march in the St. Pat's Day parade, but they won't get their hands dirty helping out their brothers over there."

"Daddy, I want to leave," Rosalie said. "Those lions are scaring me." She had climbed onto Pete's lap, and she was pressing against him, her body trembling slightly.

The lions were getting very agitated now, and they had broken out into a continuous roaring, the sound of their voices seeming to come from deep within them. They bared their long fangs and paced faster and faster, their muscles taut. The bars of their cages did not seem strong enough to hold them.

"Just a little longer," Pete said, stroking her hair. "We'll go soon, Rosalie."

"I want to go now," Rosalie said. "Please, Daddy. The lions are scaring me." She was tugging on Pete's arm, her eyes wide with terror.

Pete put his arms around her and drew her close. "Just a little longer," he whispered again. "Don't be scared. I'm here to protect you. We'll go in just a bit."

"We all have our fears, don't we?" the man in the Eagles' shirt said. "But we have to conquer them, if our brothers are to get their freedom."

"I'm doing my part," Pete said. "I'm helping out."

"To be sure, but it's not enough, is it? These are times that call for more of a commitment," the man said. "We need men who are willing to stand shoulder to shoulder with their brothers."

"What do you mean?" Pete whispered. "I'm taking three or four shipments a month. What more can I do?"

"Daddy, I'm scared," Rosalie said. Her little body was stiff with terror, her eyes as wide as saucers as she watched the lions pacing back and forth, now more rapidly than ever as the time for their feeding got closer. Pete clutched her tight, patting her hair softly.

"We need a man to deliver a package for us over there," the other man said. "Someone who can be trusted. A man like yourself."

"Me?" Pete said. "Why? Don't you have people you can trust?"

"There are many treacherous people over there who would sell out our cause," the man in the sunglasses said. "They are operating under their own flag, not ours. We have been double-crossed a number of times. We need someone we can trust. You're the lad for that."

"I can't do that," Pete said.

"And why not? It is not a difficult thing. You'd just be flying over to Dublin, where some of the lads would meet you, and then you'd go to a safe house and deliver your package. That's it. You'd be there a few days, get an idea what's going on so you can give us a report, and then you'd come home."

"I can't just fly off to Ireland," Pete said. "I have a job. I have a family. I can't get mixed up in this. You need to find someone else."

"Come on, Daddy," Rosalie said. "We need to leave now. I don't like those lions." She was pulling away from him, as if she wanted to run out of the building. He pulled her closer, but it was hard because she was trying to squirm out of his arms.

The man in the sunglasses put his hand on Pete's arm. He had a strong grip, and he tightened it so that it felt like a steel band was wrapped around Pete's forearm. "Perhaps you don't understand. You're mixed up in it already, lad. You have been for a number of years now. Now, you may think you can walk away from it, but you're mistaken, my boy. You're an accessory to a crime; I think that's what it's called. And since it involves a foreign country, I believe it's a matter that would be investigated by the FBI, perhaps even the CIA. Oh, there'd be a host of government agencies who'd want to talk to you, lad. So, you need to get your mind around the fact that you're part of this business now, and if we ask you to do something, you're going to have to do it."

"Daddy, let's go, please!" Rosalie said. Her eyes were wide and her skin was ashen, and she seemed on the verge of hysteria. The lions looked like they wanted to jump through the iron bars of their cages and come bounding into the audience. There was a zoo employee who'd just come in a side door, and he was pushing a cart with raw, bloody steaks piled high on it. The lions smelled the meat, and they were roaring and pawing at the bars of their cages.

"You come to the BOAC terminal at the airport Friday night at 6:00," the man said. "You'll be met by a man with an Eagles insignia on his jacket. He'll have a briefcase for you. It will have a full set of clothes for you, in your size, everything you need for your stay in the Republic, even down to a toothbrush. He will give you a small key that will open a secret compartment, where there will be an envelope with $100,000 in bearer bonds. You know what they are?"

"No," Pete said. "I don't." Rosalie was squirming harder now, her eyes wide with terror as she stared at the lions.

"They are payable to the bearer," the man said. "Which means they are as good as cash money. You will take the 9 PM flight to Dublin, where you will be met by a man wearing an Irish football jersey that says, "Cork United". He will take you to the safe house. You will then make your delivery, and everything will be fine."

"When do I come back?" Pete said.

"They'll tell you over there. You're getting a one-way ticket from Philadelphia. They'll buy your return ticket, and it will be up to them. They may need you to do a few more tasks for them."

"You don't know when I'm coming back?" Pete said. "That's ridiculous. I can't do this. What am I supposed to tell my boss? And my wife? I'm sorry, but you need to get another guy."

He started to stand up, but the man gripped his arm and pulled him down with surprising strength. His jacket opened just enough for Pete to see a holster and the butt of a pistol on his waist.

"Now, you listen to me," the man said, through gritted teeth. "I'm only saying this once. You are going to follow this plan to the letter, my boy, or you will suffer severe consequences. I don't care what excuse you make to your boss, or your wife. And just remember, if you don't cooperate with the lads over there, your lovely family will get a visit from some very unpleasant fellows."

"Daddy!" Rosalie screamed. "I need to go now! Please!" Her shrill voice went up an octave and seemed amplified by the tile walls. She was digging her nails into Pete's back, and he had to hold on to her tightly to keep her from climbing right over his shoulder.

The man released his grip, and smiled. "Do you understand?"

"Yes," Pete said.

"Six o'clock Friday night. The BOAC terminal. Be there."

"I will," Pete said. "Now, please, I have to go."

The keeper had thrown the first of the steaks into the lion cage, and the first lion attacked it like it was a wildebeest it had just brought down on the savannah. The other lions were roaring with blood lust now, and the echoes were so loud it made the hair on the back of Pete's neck stand up.

He took Rosalie in his arms and bolted down the steps and out the door of the lion house, pushing his way past the onlookers. By this time Rosalie was screaming hysterically, kicking her feet and sobbing. Pete was glad to get her out in the sunshine, and he ran another fifty yards when he got outside, just to get far away from the sounds of the hungry lions.

He stopped at a wooden bench and sat down, holding her close to him.

"It's okay, sweetie," he said, hugging Rosalie and stroking her hair. "It's all right now. We're out of danger now. "Then he looked up and saw Betty walking towards them, her eyes flashing, disappointment written all over her face.

CHAPTER SEVEN

June 1984

It was a brilliant early summer day, and the trees outside the bookshop were bending ever so slightly in the breeze from the river. This was Mercy's favorite time of year in New Hope, and she loved the slower summer pace, the people who came to browse along the shops, and the long summer evenings when she could sit out on her second floor porch late at night and look at the stars above the river.

She should have been happy, but the sound of Lorenzo's cough three doors down was enough to shatter her mood.

She knew his cough by heart; she had heard it every night in bed for the last two months. It was a dry, racking cough that sounded like it hurt his chest. "It's nothing," he would say. "Just a trifle, that's all." But he coughed all night long, and Mercy couldn't see how he was getting any rest.

She was worried there was something terribly wrong with him. He had circles under his eyes, and although he tried to keep up appearances, she knew it was getting harder for him to maintain his buoyantly optimistic personality.

He wouldn't see a doctor, though. "Those gentlemen are in the business of finding things wrong with a person," he'd say. "I would rather not put myself in their hands, my darling. They'll have me hooked up to all sorts of machines, and they'll be talking all that medical nonsense. I'm just a simple man from South Philadelphia, I don't want a fuss made over me."

So he went on with his days, helping out at the bookshop they'd opened ten years ago on a sunny side street of New Hope, running the projector for the screenings of old movies they showed in the back room that they'd converted to a 25 seat theater, engaging the customers in talk about movies, art, music -- all the things he loved.

These last ten years had been the happiest of Mercy's life. She'd married Lorenzo in a small ceremony at City Hall attended by his large extended family, then had a reception at a catering hall in South Philadelphia, where the food was "fit for a queen", as Lorenzo said. They were soul mates, enjoying every minute of each other's company, laughing and nuzzling and kissing like love-struck teenagers. Ten years ago when Lorenzo took her out to lunch in New Hope on a gorgeous June day like this, they'd decided on an impulse to open a bookshop and screening room, at an age when most people were retiring.

"Why not?" Lorenzo said. "I'm tired of driving that cab, but I don't want to just retire and waste away in my rocking chair. I have better things to do with my time. Let's take our money and get a lease on a property here in this beautiful little town and set up shop."

So, almost before she could think twice about it, Mercy was a bookshop owner.

It was such an idyllic life she almost thought she was dreaming. It had been ecstasy to stock the shelves, set up the screening room, decorate the store with comfortable old furniture, and become friends with the locals, who were like family to her in no time at all.

Lorenzo was in his glory, engaging in long discussions with people about all his favorite topics, and reading stacks of books. "I'm like a kid in a candy store," he'd say. "I get to order these tomes from the publishers, and then I can read them myself!" He'd give impromptu reviews to anyone who asked, and before long the customers grew to trust his judgment, seeking him out for his advice before they bought a book.

Now Mercy heard him trying to talk to the owner of the restaurant on the corner, a woman named Rosie Morley, who'd opened a bar and restaurant a few years back. She was a friendly soul with a shock of hair dyed platinum blonde and a singing voice that was like a ringing bell. Rosie had been a Big Band singer in her youth, and she often got up and sang with the bands she booked in the bar.

Lorenzo and Mercy liked to eat dinner at Rosie's place, which was called "Skibbereen", after a town in Ireland. Lorenzo called her "the woman with the golden pipes". He liked to joke around with her, and Mercy could tell he was trying to do that now, but his cough was getting in the way. He couldn't seem to get a sentence out without coughing.

There were no customers in the shop, and Mercy felt like going down to grab him and take him to the nearest doctor, but she knew he'd just brush her off with a wink and a joke.

So, she waited, listening as he ended his conversation with Rosie and walked down the street to the bookshop.

"What a beautiful day!" he said, as he came in the shop. "It's a good-to-be-alive day, isn't it?"

He came over to Mercy and kissed her on the lips, then stroked her hair tenderly. "You know, I was thinking that a day like this is just icing on the cake. I'd be happy no matter what, because I found my true love. It could be raining buckets but I'd still have a

59

smile on my face. Sunshine is a great thing, but it's not essential if you have true love."

"Are you sure you're not a poet in disguise, Mr. Antonelli?" Mercy said. "You certainly have a way with words."

"You bring out the poetry in me, Mrs. Antonelli," Lorenzo said. "I can't help myself." Then he started coughing again, and he bent double while his chest was racked with a coughing fit.

"I heard you down the street," Mercy said, when he finally stopped. You couldn't get two words out to that Rosie Morley without coughing. You really need to get that cough checked out."

"It's nothing," he said, waving his hand. "Just a little roughness in the throat, that's all. It's a family condition. I had an Uncle Dominic who coughed like this all the time. It's just in our DNA, that's all."

Mercy narrowed her eyes at him. "I don't believe you. I never heard about an Uncle Dominic in your family."

"It's true," Lorenzo said. "Although I don't know if he was a real uncle, or just a friend of the family. In my family, we never knew the full story about these things." He started to cough again, but he just talked right through it. "There are worse things in life than a little cough," he said, grinning. "Hey, it's a slow day, no customers. Why don't we just put the "Closed" sign up on the door, and go upstairs for an hour?" He came up behind Mercy and pressed against her, and nuzzled her neck the way she loved.

She found herself melting in his arms, the way she always did. It was the most amazing thing that she had a sex life now, when she had expected to be well past that. Not that her sex life had ever

60

been so hot even when she was younger. Relations with men had always been a dicey matter with her, and she'd given up on the idea of true intimacy. I'm just one of those people who's not supposed to enjoy that part of life, she thought.

But that all changed with Lorenzo. For all his intellectual curiosity he was also an earthy, passionate person, and he showed her every day in thousands of ways how much he adored her. He was constantly kissing, caressing, and hugging her, and he seemed to need to be close to her throughout the day. He was an expert lover, sensitive to her every need, and she often asked him how a bachelor like himself had ever learned so much about lovemaking.

"Oh, I just studied it, like I study everything," he said. "I like to learn things, and I made a point of learning."

"Did you have a lot of girlfriends?" she said.

"Not so many," Lorenzo said. "I had a hard time finding a woman who I could converse with. Most women weren't interested in the same things I was. Until I met you, that is." He'd give her that look that said he loved her with every fiber of his being, that he thought he was blessed to have found her, and it thrilled her every time.

Now, he had that same look, but Mercy shooed him away. "Not now," she said. "What if someone should want to buy a book while we're upstairs fooling around? That could be a customer we've lost forever."

"Oh, they'll come back," Lorenzo said. "We have an eclectic selection here, stuff you can't find anywhere else. We've cornered the market on books about Hollywood, silent films, Impressionism, sculpture, obscure tomes about philosophy, hardboiled detective stories, all that kind of stuff."

He started coughing again, and Mercy saw a look on his face that she'd seen more frequently lately -- a grayness, a hollowness in the cheeks, dark circles under his eyes. It worried her, that look, because it seemed his inexhaustible vitality was draining out of him, a thing that shocked her.

"Listen," she said. "Why don't you go upstairs and take a nap? I'll handle things down here, and if nothing's happening in an hour or so I'll come up and we can, well, have a little fun."

He smiled. "Ah, Mercy, you have quite a talent for euphemism, and it makes me giggle. Okay, I'll take you up on your offer. But you have to promise me you'll wake me up if I'm sleeping. I don't want to miss out if you're in the mood."

"I promise," Mercy said. "Now, go."

He started toward the back, where there was a door leading to the staircase. He turned when he was halfway there, and said, "Oh, I almost forgot. Do you know our friend Rosie down the street was telling me the most amazing piece of information? It seems her father was Paul Morley, who was involved with a pro-Nazi organization in World War II. I remember reading about that fellow. He gave speeches at pro-Nazi rallies in town. He spent some time in prison, as I recall."

"Morley?" Mercy said. "Did you say his name was Morley?" A shiver ran through her. She remembered her mother telling her years ago that Morley was the name her father had used before he met her. "I only found out at his funeral, when I met his first wife," her mother had said. "Who knows how many aliases that man used?"

"Yes," Lorenzo said. "Paul Morley." He turned to go, then stopped again. "You know what else? Rosie's grandfather worked for Siegmund Lubin, who made silent films. What a coincidence, huh? So did your father. I told her you'd probably want to talk to her, since you're interested in Lubin's work. Why don't we go to her restaurant for dinner tonight, listen to the entertainment, then have a chat with Rosie?" He erupted in a coughing fit, then turned and went through the door and up the stairs. Rosie heard him coughing all the way up to the second floor.

She sat down in the nearest chair and gripped the arms of it hard to stop the shaking in her body.

Morley. Lubin. It could only mean that this Rosie, who owned the bar right down the street, was the granddaughter of Mercy's father. Mercy knew him as James Francis, the man who she adored as a little girl, the light of her life, who had betrayed her mother with another woman. Maybe lots of other women. And Mercy knew, from what she had seen at his funeral, that he had had another wife before, who knew him by a different name.

What were the odds of this happening? She had thought she was over her sadness at the betrayal, the abandonment, of her father, but now it all came rushing back. The wound was still raw, it seemed, and she felt once again the yawning terror, the shock of seeing the man she adored kissing an actress on the set of one of Lubin's films. Her mother had taken Mercy and her little brother for a surprise visit to the set of the film, but it turned out to be the most shattering event in their world. None of their lives had ever been the same after that. The family was fractured, and the break was never repaired.

And now there was someone just three doors down who had a connection to this seismic event. Mercy couldn't believe it. So many conflicting emotions were tearing through her. She felt anger all over again at her father, sadness at the loss of his presence in her life, jealousy toward the woman he was kissing so many years ago, and a desire for vengeance that was surprisingly strong after all these years. A completely irrational desire came over her to go down to Rosie's bar and spit in her face. But what good would that do? Rosie had nothing to do with what her grandfather did -- she couldn't have been born when it happened. Nonetheless, Mercy had no one else to blame right now, and she wanted an outlet for her anger.

She heard Lorenzo coughing again, and she realized with chilling clarity that this was not just about her father's long-ago abandonment.

I'm afraid of being abandoned again, she thought.

CHAPTER EIGHT

"Okay, here's a particular favorite of mine," Rosie said to the crowd. It was a Thursday night crowd in early June, not too packed, but plenty of locals and some new faces, come to hear Rosie sing some jazz standards, mixed in with her interpretations of doo wop songs, like she did every Thursday night.

The pianist, a professorial looking man with glasses named Ted Wainwright, nodded to the upright bass player and the drummer.

They launched into "You're The Top," the Cole Porter song, and Rosie went through Cole Porter's catalogue of 1930s names from the news:

You're the top!

You're Mahatma Gandhi.

You're the top!

You're Napoleon Brandy.

You're the purple light

Of a summer night in Spain,

You're the National Gallery

You're Garbo's salary,

You're cellophane.

You're sublime,

You're turkey dinner,

You're the time, the time of a Derby winner

I'm a toy balloon that's fated soon to pop

But if, baby, I'm the bottom,

You're the top!

She was always happiest when she was singing, and tonight was no different. She tossed her head and snapped her fingers on every beat, and threw her whole body into the rhythms of the song. She felt joy in every fiber of her being, and it was the same joy she'd felt as a teenager singing big band songs at the USO in Philadelphia, but now she was a fiftyish woman who owned a bar in New Hope, Pennsylvania and she had a man looking at her from a table near the front of the room who lit her up every time he was near her.

It was Jack Caldwell, and he'd been a blessing from the first day he walked into her life, five years ago when she'd seen him on the porch of this very hotel. There had been a spark then, and there was still a spark now, every time she saw his tousled hair and the smile lines around his eyes and mouth, his strong yet supple hands and the way he filled out the bomber jackets he liked to wear.

He was smiling now, but Rosie knew what the smile meant. "Why do you sing those old songs from the 1930s?" he would tell her after she came down off the stage. "They're relics of another age. Who remembers Greta Garbo? Is she still alive? Come on, Rosie, join the modern world."

He would smile when he said it, and Rosie always had the same rejoinder. "The trouble with you is you don't recognize a classic song when you hear it. Cole Porter has a hell of a lot more to say to me than Billy Idol, or whoever the latest pop superstar is."

Jack liked to pretend that the past was dead, that it should be no concern of hers. "The future, Rosie, that's what you need to focus on. Change is coming, and it's going to be like nothing we've ever experienced."

He was still a futurist, and he worked for major corporations, using his house on a hill overlooking the Delaware River as a home base. He flew out to California several times a month, and he always came back with some new story of exciting things that were happening out there.

Rosie respected his intelligence. She'd taken his advice and bought stock in a company called Apple a few years before, and she'd made a healthy profit on it. After that she took his recommendations about other stocks she should put her money into, and each time she made a tidy profit it enabled her to do some more work on the Skibbereen Hotel, her place here in New Hope. She'd expand the kitchen, hire a better chef, book better entertainment, and redo the bar. It was an adventure, and she was grateful to Jack for giving her the means to do this.

Truth be told, Jack was the reason she'd bought the place. The day she met him she knew there was something special between them, and she didn't want to let it slip away. After her visit to the psychic, who told her she was trapped in the past, she decided she had gotten too comfortable, too afraid of change, and she was going to break out of her self-imposed prison and do something impulsive again. She went back to the abandoned hotel after her session with the crystal ball, and she found Jack loitering around the place again.

"What are you doing back here?" he said. "I thought you were going back to your oldies records."

"I'm going to buy this place," she said, surprised to hear the words coming out of her mouth. "I always wanted to have a place where I could serve food and drinks, and sing once in awhile. I used to sing at a USO during the war, and I have fond memories of that place. Yes, I'm going to buy it."

He smiled. "Well, that's great. You can probably get it cheap, because it's falling apart, but do you have the financing? It's going to take money to fix this place up, you know."

"I can get money," Rosie said, trying to hide her uncertainty with bravado. "I darn sure can. No problem."

"I see," he said. "And what are you going to do, sell those oldies records? How much will that bring in?"

"More than you think," Rosie said. Her bravado was fading as she looked at the broken floorboards, peeling paint, and cracked windows. He was right; it was going to take a lot of money to fix this place up. What was she thinking? It was a crazy idea to buy it.

"Good," he said. "But just in case it doesn't bring in enough, I'll go in on this as your partner. I have some money put away, and I've always wanted to open a place like this. I guess that's why I keep hanging around here. It attracts me. And, by the way, I'm good at fixing things. I'm not just a brilliant thinker, you know. I'm pretty good with my hands."

And he was. The one thing about Jack Caldwell, he was full of surprises. He had an insatiable curiosity, and he loved learning things. Besides computers, technology, physics, and a host of other scientific disciplines, he knew practical things, everything from carpentry to cooking to how tune up a car. "The word for me is 'polymath'," he'd say. "I just like learning things."

They pooled their money and Rosie borrowed some money from the Dittybopper, and when they still didn't have enough they canvassed the banks in Bucks County till they found one that was willing to lend them some more. Rosie and Jack did the renovation work themselves whenever they could, and when they needed expert help they bartered services with the local tradesmen. Rosie would offer to sing at weddings and bar mitzvahs, and Jack would do the cooking for the affair. Or, he'd build a computer from scratch for a local electrician, all the while regaling the man with stories about the amazing changes that were on the horizon.

They started out small at first, with just a modest bar and a restaurant that opened for lunch and dinner. Rosie was in her element, though, singing impromptu snatches of songs, playing records until she could afford to hire musicians, telling jokes and flirting with the customers. The place was an instant magnet for the town, and it was crowded with customers from the start. When the money started flowing in, Rosie used it to keep expanding, until now it took up almost a whole block. She had a full-scale restaurant, a bar with a stage for the entertainment, and she was even renting out the old hotel rooms upstairs, after she redecorated and filled them with antiques. She lived on the top floor, converting it into a suite of rooms for herself, and her pride and joy was the rooftop deck that looked out over the Delaware River to the town of Lambertville in New Jersey, where she'd sit with Jack late at night after the bar was closed, talking of "cabbages and kings" as Jack liked to say, quoting the Walrus in "Alice In Wonderland".

Jack Caldwell had been good for her. He was a calm, steady presence, always ready to laugh or tease her good-naturedly, an artist with his hands and a great conversationalist. He encouraged her at every step of the way in this venture, and his confidence in her made her feel like she was blooming right before his eyes. He had a restless spirit, always looking for new challenges, and it was infectious. She realized she had been stuck in a rut for so long before she met him. Now, he had helped her open a new chapter in her life.

She finished the Cole Porter song, acknowledged the audience applause, and said, "Now I'll let this wonderful trio continue with some of their original compositions. Enjoy!"

She stepped off the stage and walked over to Jack's table, stopping to say hello to some of the regulars on the way.

Rosie hadn't noticed before, but Jack was sitting with the owners of the Hollywood and Vine bookshop that was down the street from her place. They were a sweet older couple named Mercy and Lorenzo, and she had had many conversations with them in the last few years. Lorenzo was a lot like Jack, he seemed interested in a wide variety of subjects, and he'd often engage Jack in conversations about arcane subjects that he'd been reading about. Jack would order books that he was interested in, and Lorenzo would often read them as soon as they were delivered, then bring the books down to Jack and ask a myriad of questions about them.

Lorenzo had been by just this afternoon, and he'd had a conversation with Rosie about Mercy's father. It seemed by some strange coincidence that he had worked for the same silent filmmaker in the early years of the 20th century, a man named Siegmund Lubin, as Rosie's grandfather. Lorenzo thought that was quite an astonishing fact, and he said he'd bring Mercy around to talk about it further. "You two could be related somehow," he'd said.

Rosie hadn't thought much about it, because she didn't know very much about her grandfather Peter Morley, and anyway that was such a long time ago. But there they were, Mercy and Lorenzo, sitting with Jack, and Mercy had a look on her face that seemed like worry mixed with anticipation.

"Hi, folks," Rosie said, sitting down. "I'm so glad you came in tonight. Did you enjoy the set?"

"You sound like an angel, as usual," Lorenzo said. "Absolutely beautiful. I don't know why you're not an international star, Rosie."

"Stop or you'll make me blush," Rosie said. "I'm just average, that's all. Besides, I don't sing the popular stuff. Jack likes to say I'm stuck in the past."

"Nonsense," Lorenzo said. "Those are the classic songs you sing. They'll never go out of style."

"At least she gave up most of that Fifties stuff," Jack said. "Now she's singing Cole Porter songs. She's moving backward in time."

"I love it," Mercy said. "Those songs are eternal."

71

"That's why you two are my favorite customers," Rosie said, smiling. "Can I get you a drink? It's on me. Everybody except you," she said, nudging Jack in the shoulder.

"We're fine," Lorenzo said. "I'm happy with my water, and Mercy has a glass of wine." He started coughing, and he took a drink of water to quell his cough. "But anyway," he continued, "I brought Mercy in tonight because of our conversation this afternoon."

"Yes," Rosie said. "Small world, isn't it? It's such a coincidence that we have relatives who worked for that guy who made silent films."

"It's amazing," Mercy said, leaning forward. She seemed more intense than usual, hanging on every word. "Lorenzo said your grandfather worked for Lubin? What was his name?"

"It was Morley," Rosie said. "Peter Morley."

Mercy exhaled heavily, as if someone had punched her in the stomach. Lorenzo put his hand on her forearm and his eyes looked worried. "What's the matter?" he said. "Do you know that name?"

Mercy nodded her head. "He was my father."

CHAPTER NINE

"Peter Morley was your father?" Rosie said. She looked at the white haired woman sitting across from her, and didn't know whether to laugh or cry. She had gotten to know Mercy a bit over the years, but only as one business owner to another. She knew Mercy and her husband Lorenzo were deeply in love, holding hands when they took walks after they closed the bookstore at night, laughing at each other's jokes as they sipped espresso in the local coffee shop, and celebrating each other's birthdays by decorating the store with balloons and flowers.

She thought they were two sweet older people, and she enjoyed seeing them around town, but that was the extent of it. Now it seemed bizarre that she and Rosie were somehow related, and she couldn't accept it at first.

"I think you must be wrong," she said. "I don't know much about my grandfather, but I know enough to think we're not related. He was named Peter Morley, that's true. He was an immigrant from Ireland. He had three sons, including my father. The other two sons died, and my Dad was the only one who had children. I don't remember hearing about a sister."

"I guess you'd call me a stepsister," Mercy said. "I was born to your grandfather's second wife. He left your grandmother with those three sons, just walked out on her. He started calling himself James Francis, and he met my mother and made up a completely new history for himself. My mother's name was Edith, and she was from England. He married her and had two children with her. I'm one of those children."

73

Rosie was flabbergasted. "This is hard for me to believe. I mean, do you have proof?"

Lorenzo put his hand on Mercy's and squeezed it. He seemed to think this was going to be very hard for her. He leaned over and said: "Her mother found out the truth at the funeral. Edith, Mercy's mother, threw her husband out when she found that he had a roving eye. You know, he was one of those gentlemen who can't resist a pretty girl."

"My parents weren't living together at the time he died," Mercy said. "I took my mother to the funeral, and we met his first wife. I remember meeting your father, Paul Morley, and your grandmother Rose. We never knew he had been married before."

"You met my grandmother?" Rosie said. "I still find this hard to believe." She folded her arms, and said: "Tell, me, what did she look like?"

"Oh, she was a tall white-haired woman with green eyes and an Irish lilt to her voice," Mercy said. "And your father was very kind, a very kind gentleman. He looked like he had suffered a lot. I met your mother, too. She was a beautiful woman, a petite Scottish lass with auburn hair."

Rosie put her hand over her mouth. The combo on the stage was playing a jazzy version of a Gershwin tune, and she was tapping her foot under the table to the beat, but she felt like someone had punched her in the stomach. She realized from the details of the story that Mercy was telling the truth. She remembered as a little girl the strange man with white hair who'd died on her parents' front porch, and she recalled her father telling her that the dead man was her grandfather. She had refused to accept that, and she told her father that this man couldn't possibly be her grandfather. Her

74

parents didn't take her to the funeral, but she remembered hearing her father and her grandmother talking that night about another family that had shown up. She had a dim recollection of listening at the top of the stairs when she was supposed to be in bed, hearing them say the name "James Francis" and talking about a woman named Edith.

She reached over and embraced Mercy, feeling as if her heart was ready to burst. Mercy was crying softly, and Rosie couldn't hold her own tears back. Even Lorenzo seemed to be filling up with emotion. Jack wasn't as comfortable with scenes like this, and he made an excuse to get up and get more drinks at the bar. Rosie took his seat and moved closed to Mercy, putting her arm around the older woman's shoulder.

"I can't believe it," she said, wiping tears from her eyes with a tissue. "I can't believe at my age I'm discovering a big sister."

"It's wonderful, isn't it?" Lorenzo said, blinking back tears. "Life is just full of surprises." He coughed, a dry racking cough that sounded like a smoker's hack, although Rosie had never seen him with a cigarette in his mouth.

"It certainly is," Rosie said. "You know, I was just a kid when my grandfather died, but I remember the adults talking about what a rascal he was. I didn't understand it, but now I do. Did you know him very well?" she asked Mercy.

Mercy smiled. "He was my hero. I thought the sun rose and set on him. I was the only daughter he had, and he doted on me. He used to take me out to the country for picnics, and ice-skating in Fairmount Park in the winter, and to the zoo on Sundays. He was a very charming man, and he lit up a room when he walked into it. And he had the most beautiful singing voice." She stopped, and she grinned broadly. "Why, Rosie, I bet that's where you got your beautiful voice. Your grandfather was a terrific singer."

"Was he?" Rosie said. "I wish I could have heard him sing."

Lorenzo slapped the table and said: "Why, you can! You can hear him sing."

"How?" Rosie said. "He died a long time ago, and I'm sure there are no recordings."

"Not true," Lorenzo said, smiling at Mercy. "We were lucky enough to come into possession of an old gramophone recording he made, probably back around the time of the First World War, and we have it tucked away at our house. It's an amazing thing, to hear his voice coming out of that old record player. Do you want to hear it?"

"Of course I do!" Rosie said.

"Well, then, let's go hear it," Lorenzo said, standing up.

"Where are you going?" Jack Caldwell said. He had just brought back glasses of wine for the table, but now it appeared they were on their way out.

"We're going to hear my grandfather sing," Rosie said. "Come on, it's from about 70 years ago. Isn't that amazing?"

Jack grinned sarcastically. "Oh, I'll bet the sound is crystal clear. They certainly had great recording technology back then."

"Stop with your futurist stuff for just once, will you?" Rosie said, punching him in the shoulder. "Come on, it's an artifact, a piece of living history. You have to admit that's special. Just put those glasses down and let's go."

They all piled out the door and went down the street to Mercy and Lorenzo's bookstore, and Lorenzo unlocked the door and led them through the store and then up the back stairs to the living quarters above. Mercy made them coffee while Lorenzo searched in a closet for the vintage gramophone, then he opened a steamer trunk and took out a large black platter from a case, and said, "Here it is. Prepare to be amazed."

He lifted the gramophone onto the coffee table, placed the platter carefully on it, wound it up vigorously, and put the stylus on it. Immediately there was the sound of a man singing, in a high Irish tenor, a voice of such sweetness yet with a ragged edge to it, a yearning and almost a desperation to it.

Oh father dear, I oft-times hear you speak of Erin's isle

Her lofty hills, her valleys green, her mountains rude and wild

They say she is a lovely land wherein a saint might dwell

So why did you abandon her, the reason to me tell?

Oh son, I loved my native land with energy and pride

Till a blight came o'er the praties; my sheep, my cattle died

My rent and taxes went unpaid, I could not them redeem

And that's the cruel reason why I left old Skibbereen.

77

Rosie felt herself choking up. It brought tears to her eyes, to realize that this achingly sweet voice was her grandfather, a man she'd met only once in her life, a man who'd had two families and two names, and who knows how many secrets?

When the last notes had faded away, Rosie said: "What is that song he sang? It's so beautiful and sad."

"It's a song about the Irish potato famine, in the 1840s," Mercy said. "There's a town called Skibbereen in southern Ireland, and the famine was very bad there. Lots of people starved to death. He was born twenty years after the famine, but it affected people for generations. He probably lost aunts and uncles to it. You can hear the pain in his voice, can't you?"

"Yes," Rosie said. "It's like his heart is breaking. Did he talk about the famine with you?"

Mercy laughed. "Oh, no. He didn't say a word about that. He never told us anything about Ireland, not a thing. I always wondered why he didn't want to talk about the past much. It was because he had another family, of course, but I didn't know that till years later.

"My father didn't talk about him either," Rosie said. "We knew our grandmother, Rose, very well, but my Dad would change the subject whenever I asked about my grandfather. 'Oh, it's too complicated for you to understand,' he'd say. I'll tell you all about it some other time.' He never did, though. I wish I knew more about my family history."

"What did your grandmother say about him?" Mercy said. "Didn't she tell you anything?"

"No, she got remarried, to a man named Martin Lancaster, and she never told me about her first husband."

"What did you say?" Jack said, sitting bolt upright on the couch. "Did you say 'Martin Lancaster'? Is that what I heard you say?"

"Yes," Rosie said. "Martin was my step-grandfather."

"Wow, this is amazing," Jack said. "I don't know if I'd believe this if I didn't know it was happening." He looked like he'd just had a major shock to his system.

"Jack, stop talking in riddles," Rosie said, "and tell us what this is all about. You look like one of your predictions about the future is wrong, and you have egg on your face."

"Well, it's a pretty amazing thing," he said. "I'm related to Martin Lancaster."

CHAPTER TEN

"What?" Rosie said. "How do you know that? And how do you know it's the same Martin Lancaster?"

"Let me ask you one question," Jack said. "Do you know if your grandmother Rose was an domestic servant when she came to this country? Did she work for a wealthy family in Philadelphia?"

"Yes," Rosie said. "She used to talk about it. She called them 'the foin people, who lived in a grand big house'. She said it was in Chestnut Hill, on the edge of the city."

Jack shook his head. "I can't believe it. This is incredible."

"What?" Rosie said. "You know them?"

"They were my mother's people," he said. "The Lancasters were my grandparents. They lived in a big house in Chestnut Hill. The father made his money as an attorney for the Pennsylvania Railroad. They had servants, and your grandmother was one of them. So was your grandfather."

"How do you know all this?" Rosie said. "You never told me you grew up rich."

"I didn't," Jack said. "I grew up middle class, in New Jersey. I didn't know about the Lancaster connection till my mother was dying in the 1960s. She gave me a box with photos, letters, and documents in it. I found out that she was the child of Victoria Lancaster, Martin's sister. This Victoria was a real radical for her time, a progressive woman who espoused free love, atheism, and revolution, and her family was horrified by her. She lived in New York with her anarchist boyfriend, and at some point she got pregnant. The child was my mother, who came to be known as Annie. Victoria wasn't interested in being a mother, so she was going to abort the baby. The Lancasters found out and arranged for her to go away and have the baby, but they took it and shipped it off to a cousin in New Jersey, and Victoria was allowed to go back to her life in New York. It was all hushed up, and my mother didn't know anything about it till years later, when Mrs. Lancaster told her before she died."

For the second time tonight, Rosie felt like she'd been punched in the stomach. She felt like the oxygen in the room had been sucked out, and she was fighting to get a breath.

"Are you sure about this?" she said. "It's so bizarre. Why did Mrs. Lancaster tell your mother?"

"I don't know," Jack said. "I suppose she felt sorry for my mother, that she didn't know the truth. By that time the Lancasters had their share of tragedy, you know. Their son Tom had died young, Victoria died in the flu epidemic of 1919, the father died suddenly a few years later, and then Mrs. Lancaster lost just about everything in the stock market crash of 1929. She used to come and visit my mother in New Jersey, pretending to be my mother's aunt. She finally confessed in the late 1930s, before she died. It must have affected my mother deeply, because she didn't tell me the truth until she was near the end of her life."

"That's quite a story," Lorenzo said. He coughed, then sipped his coffee. "It just goes to show, the past never releases its hold on us. People try to run away from it, but they can't."

"I learned that lesson," Mercy said. "I tried to blot out the memory of my father for most of my adult life. And yet he still came back through that," she nodded to the gramophone. "To speak to me."

"Yeah," Jack said. "I think my mother wanted to know more about the Lancasters. She had newspaper clippings, obituaries, etc., in that box she gave me. Even a picture of their old house in Chestnut Hill. I don't know why I still have all that stuff. I carted it all around the country with me, every time I moved. I used to tell myself I was going to throw it away, but I never did. Guess it's a good thing I didn't."

"You know," Rosie said, "I'd like to see that house. Is it still there?"

There was an enormous craving inside of her now, all of a sudden, to see the house where her grandmother had worked as a young woman.

And where she'd met Rosie's grandfather.

Jack frowned. "It's still there," he said. "But why would you want to see it? It's just a house, a pile of stones where your grandparents lived, probably a hundred years ago. I don't see any point in visiting it."

"I don't know," Rosie said. "I just have a feeling that I want to see it."

"Oh, is this one of your psychic moments?" Jack said, sarcastically. "Are you feeling that the spirits are calling you there?" he teased.

"I don't know," Rosie said, refusing to be drawn in. "I just feel strongly that I want to see it. To walk through it, if we can. It's part of my family history, Jack, and yours too. Why wouldn't you want to see it?"

"Yes," Lorenzo said. "I think it would be a great thing to walk through a house that my grandparents lived in so many years ago. Mine came from a little village in Italy that was destroyed in World War II, so there's nothing left for me to visit. If there's a house still standing where your grandparents lived, you should visit it while you can."

"It could turn out badly," Jack said. "I don't know who lives there, or what condition the house is in. It's an hour drive from here, and you could be very disappointed when you get there."

Lorenzo coughed. "I'm sure Rosie can handle disappointment. What's important is that she gets a chance to see the house where her grandparents live. Don't you understand, Jack? It's a connection, a link to the past."

"He doesn't care about the past," Rosie said.

"That's wrong," Jack said. "Actually, I do care about the past. I just think the future is more interesting. I don't see the point in going to visit that house."

"Are you afraid the current owners won't let us in?" Rosie said.

"Not at all," Jack said. "As a matter of fact, I've met the man who owns it now. I was at a tech conference in Philadelphia a couple of years ago, and I met him. He's a History professor at the University of Pennsylvania, but he's one of those big picture thinkers like me, and he has an interest in technology. We were eating lunch one day when he told me where he lived, and I figured out it was the same house that was owned by the Lancasters at the turn of the century. I don't think he'd mind at all if we went there; he'd probably give us a tour himself."

"That's great," Lorenzo said, turning to Rosie. "You should do this."

"I will," Rosie said. "The sooner the better. When can we go, Jack?"

"Excuse me," Mercy said. "I would like to go also. That is, if you don't mind me coming along. That house is part of my family history too. I would love to see where my father worked as a young man."

"Of course," Rosie said. "I wouldn't think of going without you."

Lorenzo coughed again. "And me too? I love to look at old houses."

"Let me think about it," Jack said, suddenly turning serious. "You know I don't believe in that psychic stuff, Rosie, but something about this gives me an uneasy feeling. I don't know if it's a good idea."

CHAPTER ELEVEN

"This has certainly been an interesting night," Mercy said after Jack and Rosie left. "It seems I can never get away from my dear father. Everywhere I go around here there are connections to him. That's why I moved to the West Coast originally, but now I'm back and he seems to be everywhere."

She was sitting on the couch where she could look out her window at the lights across the river in Lambertville. It was her favorite spot in the house, and she liked to see the changing patterns of the leaves on the trees, the changing colors and movements of the river, and the sparkling lights at night.

Lorenzo was sitting next to her, drinking a glass of water, trying to stifle his cough again. "We're all connected to the people who came before us," he said. "Americans don't revere their ancestors the way the Asian cultures do, but that's a mistake. We act like we have no history, like we just appeared here out of nothing. We should give our forebears more respect. I'm sure your father was an amazing man." He coughed twice, and took a sip of water.

Mercy looked at him with concern. "Why won't you go to the doctor?" she said.

"Oh, they just want to fill you full of pills," he said. "I think the body has a marvelous healing mechanism in it, and we just need to trust it. I'll get better, don't worry."

"No you won't," Mercy said.

Lorenzo looked at her with surprise. "What do you mean, darling?"

"You're not going to get better, I know it," she said, with force. "You are not. You are sick with something serious, Lorenzo. It's cancer, I know it, and you're going to leave me. I waited my whole life to find someone like you, you've done so much for me, and now you're going to leave me. Just like my father did."

She put her hand over her mouth and started crying, and her body shook with the sobs.

Lorenzo put his arm around her, soothing her. "Don't say that, Mercy. Why, that's the furthest thing from the truth. I'm not going anywhere, believe it. I was looking for you my whole life too -- you're not the only one who made out in this relationship."

Then he kissed her, and Mercy felt once again the rightness of it, the special sweetness of his lips on hers. She had never felt that way with a man, ever, and it was more than sexual passion. There was a benediction, a grace, in it, something that swept away all her fears and the guilt and shame over her father's betrayal so many years ago. The wound in her heart was healed whenever she was around Lorenzo. He was such a gentle but strong lover, someone who completed her in every way. She felt such peace, such happiness when she was in his arms at moments like this. Lorenzo ran his fingers through her hair, and he pulled her closer. She could feel the warmth of his body, his strong arms holding her close, and she relaxed into them. It was so peaceful, so secure. She was so lucky she found him.

Lorenzo pulled his lips from hers, and he looked at her with such tenderness. "You have been the best thing that ever happened to me," he said. "You have given me so much happiness, and I thank you for it." He started coughing again, and before Mercy could bring up doctors and tests again, he said, "Excuse me, I'm going to get another glass of water."

He got up from the couch, and Mercy smiled at him. "You are my hero," she said.

He smiled. "And you are my queen. I'll be right back."

He went in the kitchen and poured himself a glass of water from the pitcher they kept in the refrigerator. He took a long drink and it cooled the rawness in his throat. He saw his reflection in the window above the kitchen sink and said, low enough that Mercy couldn't hear: "You'd better get this checked out, my friend. Tomorrow."

He went back in the other room, a feeling of such peace inside, the sure knowledge that his life had truly been blessed since he met this wonderful woman.

He looked at her on the couch, her head tilted back and a smile on her face, eyes looking at the ceiling, and knew instantly that she was gone.

CHAPTER TWELVE

April 11, 1987

Pete:

I'm sending this letter to the address you gave me, and I hope you get it. I have no idea where you are, except that you're somewhere in Ireland. That's what I had to tell our children when they asked where you were on Sunday. "Daddy is somewhere in Ireland," I had to say. "He's there on business." Luke is still young enough to accept that explanation, but Rosalie is almost eight now, and she didn't buy it for a minute. "Nobody should be on business on a Sunday," she said. "He should be home eating Grandma's dinner with us."

I didn't know what to tell her, Pete. I'm not good at lying, and she'd see right through any story I told her. We had Sunday dinner at my mother's house, and my family did their best to keep her distracted, but she had tears in her eyes when I put her to bed that night.

She needs her Daddy, Pete, and so does Marty. What I don't understand is that you told me all those stories about how hard it was when your mother ran off to London back in the Sixties. I know you felt lonely and abandoned, and you're still so angry with her that you won't even speak to her all these years later. I thought that meant you'd never do the same thing to your children, but you're repeating what she did right now.

Oh, sure, you're not gone as long as she was; you spend weeks, even months with us. But you always leave again, and I never know for how long you'll be away.

And even when you're with us, you seem distracted these days. You're a ball of nerves, Pete, always clenching your jaw and balling up your fists, and you seem like you're ready to fight at a moment's notice. You're so angry about so many things!

Mostly it's the Troubles in Ireland, and I understand how that means something to you, since your family came from there. But, Pete, you're an American, not an Irish citizen, and you have family and a life over here! I feel sorry for the Catholics who are suffering oppression over there, but there's a lot of oppression over here to worry about too.

You know as well as I do that my people haven't fared so well, that we have our share of problems. Dr. King only got things started in the 1960s -- there's still plenty of racism in this country, and African Americans are suffering every day because of it. I see the way people look at my children in the supermarket, or on the street. Mixed race children still have a hard time even now, in the 1980s. These children need somebody to stand up for them, Pete. I can't be the strong one all the time.

I get so tired, Pete. I went back to practicing law because I wanted to use my degree to help people, and it gives me satisfaction to do that. But I fight with people all day long, and then I come home and have to fight with you when you're here, or handle all the parenting when you're not. Do you understand how hard that is?

My mother didn't want me to marry you, you know that. She thought it would be too hard for a mixed race couple today. But I'm stubborn, I admit it, and I thought our love could withstand any challenge. Sometimes now I'm not so sure. I still love you, Baby, but it's hard when you're full of so much anger.

I know it's because of the Vietnam War, and all the things you saw over there. I remember when I first met you, when you came home from Vietnam to give me my fiancée Calvin's letter, how angry you looked on the front porch at my mother's house. My mother called you, "that angry white boy" when she came out to the kitchen to tell me you had asked for me. "You watch yourself with that angry white boy," she said. "You stand right at the front door, and don't be sitting out the porch with that boy. He looks dangerous."

I didn't pay her any mind, because I saw a gentleness in your eyes. I guess it was something soft behind the anger, something that was wounded and lost. My mother thought I was crazy to get mixed up with you, even years later when we met again and I was out of law school. She thought it would bring no good to date you, and I guess she still wonders what's going on with us. I'm not saying she doesn't like you -- she adores you, you know that -- but she thinks we've chosen a hard road for ourselves, getting married and having kids, when there's still so much prejudice in this world.

I believe in us, Pete, I always have. I thought if anybody could make it, we could. I think we're terrific together, and I just put all that other racial stuff in the background when I see you, when you're holding me in your arms. Baby, it's still the sweetest thing when you kiss me.

But it's hard, Pete, it's hard. I'm getting pulled in so many different directions. You're away so much, off on your adventures or whatever it is you're doing over there, and I'm home with our two kids, trying to juggle my career and being there to give them kisses and hugs and the tenderness they need from both of us. My mother loves you, but there are people in my family, and some of my friends, who keep telling me I'm a fool for putting up with this. They tell me you're taking advantage of me, and sometimes they do it in language that I'm not happy about. Oh, I tell them pretty fast to cut it out when they start with that stuff, but I still hear those voices in my head at night when I'm all alone, telling me I'm crazy for staying with you.

I don't know how much longer I can stand it, Pete. I think you're going to have to make some decisions, and you'd better think long and hard about this. I want to have a husband who's next to me in bed, and a father to my children who's going to be there for them when this world knocks them down, because you know it will. I am not going to keep on lying to my children about where their father is, no matter how noble the cause is. And have you ever thought about how irresponsible you're being? I know you're putting yourself in danger, even if you don't tell me exactly what's going on. I've heard some bad things about that Larry Flynn guy you're always hanging around with at the bar. He smells like trouble, as my mother used to say, and I think he's got you mixed up in some things that are dangerous.

I'm asking you to think about this, Pete, and give me an answer. I expect you to be home in two weeks at the latest, and I want you to tell me what your priorities are. If you can't tell me you're quitting this Irish business, then I think you'd better move out. It hurts me to say that, Pete, but that's the way it's got to be, for both of us.

And the children.

Love,

Betty

Pete folded the letter and put it in his pocket. He felt a stab of sadness in his throat, but he dulled it with a drink of the strong Irish whiskey he had in the shot glass in front of him, then put the glass down and looked at Seamus McGarran, his Irish handler.

"A letter from home is it?" McGarran said. "I hope everything is all right."

"No it's not," Pete said. "It's not right at all."

They were sitting in a pub in the village of Bundoran, just over the border of Northern Ireland, in County Sligo, in the Republic of Ireland. It was early evening, and the pub was nearly empty. Pete and McGarran were sitting in front of half-eaten bowls of stew.

"'Tis a pity," McGarran said. "Families do not always understand our struggle, do they?"

"No," Pete said. "Sometimes I don't either, though." He motioned to the bartender to pour him another drink, but McGarran waved the bartender off and touched Pete on the shoulder.

"I don't think you should be having another," McGarran said. "We have important business to discuss tonight, and Looney will want us clearheaded."

"I was told I could go home to America soon," Pete said. "I don't want to go to this meeting. I've been away too long. Maybe you don't understand, but I have a family."

"Oh, family's a wonderful thing, isn't it?" McGarran said. "I've got family meself, you know. Sure, I've got a wife and a little lad of three. He's a fine young fellow, name of Pearse, after Patrick Pearse, of course. One of the greatest Irish freedom fighters, he was. Family's what we're fighting for, lad. So that our sons and daughters can live in a free Ireland. All of it, free, not just the south."

"Yes, but violence doesn't solve problems, it only creates more of them," Pete said. "I thought I learned that lesson in Vietnam. I can't believe I'm right back in the middle of a war again. When I got out of the Army I didn't want to ever see a gun for the rest of my life."

"Now, don't go getting soft on us," McGarran said. "You need to remember all the innocent Catholics who've been killed in this conflict, all because they were Irish and the wrong religion. We need to keep up the pressure on those bastards in Belfast and London, or we'll never get a free Ireland. They'll keep our brothers up north under the English boot heel for another five centuries."

"That's the problem," Pete said. "Innocent people get killed on both sides. Once you bring the guns and the bombs out it has to happen."

Just then the door opened and Jim Looney walked in, with his weaselly-faced lieutenant, Con Wilson. Looney was a big, ruddy man with a huge head, the frame of a bear, and a smile like pure sunshine when he wanted to use it. He could turn from playful jokiness to cold menace in an instant, though. He was said to have personally killed more than a dozen British soldiers, and quite a few Loyalists to boot. He was running the show in this part of Ireland for the Provisional Irish Republican Army, and he had called a meeting for tonight with Pete and McGarran to discuss something important.

"Ho, there's my Yank," he said, coming over and slapping Pete on the back. "What's the matter, boy? You're looking a bit long in the face."

"Oh, he's fine, Jim," McGarran said. "Just a little homesick, I'd say."

"Homesick are you?" Looney said. "Well, that's something I can understand. I'm from Kinsale myself, way down in the south. I don't like the weather up here at all -- too cold and rainy for my taste. But, we all must make sacrifices, right lad?"

He slapped Pete on the back again, and Pete was overcome by a wave of anger. All of a sudden he had an urge to pick up his glass and break it over Looney's head. It was a wave of irrational crimson energy that rippled through his body, and he had to grip the bar with both hands to keep from doing it.

McGarran must have noticed it, for he immediately said, "Now, Jim, we can't be tarrying here all night, you know. You called us here to discuss something, and we'd like to get down to it."

"Right," Looney said. "Follow me, lads."

He led the way past the bar and down a narrow corridor to a back room where there was a rickety old wooden table and some chairs scattered about. There was a peat fire burning in a stone fireplace, but the room still felt drafty and cold.

"Sorry for the accommodations, lads," Looney said, pulling a chair up to the table and motioning for the others to do as well. "I wish we could be having lunch at the Ritz in Dublin, but this is the best I can do at the moment."

"What is this about?" Pete snapped. "We've been waiting for you for two hours."

Looney chuckled. "Well, well, you Yanks certainly don't waste any time, do you?"

"Perhaps he'd like a drink," Con Wilson said. "To calm him down. He seems a bit jittery."

He smiled, but it was a smile of malice. He was known as a treacherous man, and his smile inspired no confidence in others.

"No, no," Looney said. "No drinks. I need clear heads, Con, clear heads." He cleared his throat. "Now, here's what we're here to discuss. Things have been heating up lately, as you know. There was that Anglo Irish Agreement a year or so back that inspired some hope in us that we were finally making progress. The Brits actually agreed to let the politicians in Dublin have some say in what happens in the North."

"Yes," McGarran said. "I think they were finally seeing the light."

"Maybe," Looney said. "Whatever the case, the Loyalists didn't like it at all, and they're showing their displeasure through the barrel of a gun. There's been a rash of attacks on our people, and it's time to retaliate. We must strike back."

"It's a vicious cycle," Pete said. "Action and reaction. That's what war is, why it keeps going on, century after century. It never solves anything, just keeps the cycle going."

"Tell me, lad, are you actually sympathizing with the Brits?" Looney said. He was smiling, but he also had a look of suspicion in his eyes.

"No," Pete said. "I just like to be clear about things. Nothing happens in a vacuum."

"It seems we have a military philosopher here," Looney said, winking at Wilson and McGarran. "A man who likes to think about the ultimate meaning of war."

He leaned closer, his face inches from Pete's. "Now, all that philosophizing is a fine thing, but I wonder if it will take away your balls, my boy. Because I need men who don't think, they just do what's necessary. There's no time for philosophy, for moralizing, when you're staring down the barrel of a gun."

Pete gripped the table, once again wanting to smash Looney in the face, but reining in his rage with a massive effort.

"Don't you worry about me," he said, his voice low and calm. "I've been in combat, Mr. Looney. I know what it's like to have bullets whistling past your head. To see your best friend's head get blown off and explode like a cantaloupe that's been dropped off a tall building. To kill someone when you're close enough to see the fear in their eyes. I know all that, Mr. Looney, and that's why I have reservations about doing it again."

"Well," Looney said. "That's a pretty situation to be in. I thought you said he was our man, McGarran. Now I'm wondering if he's only here because of the money he owes to our friends in the States. I don't see any fire in his eyes. The man's a mercenary, and he'll run at the first sign of trouble, that's what I think."

"He's our man," McGarran piped up. "Don't you worry about that, Jim. I've seen Pete in action, and there's not a cooler head out there. He's got ice water in his veins, Jim. Don't worry about him. Why, just last week he beat up someone we suspected of stealing money from the treasury. You should have seen him then, Jim, the way he whacked the stuffing out of that thieving bastard. He's just a little irritated with waiting around, is all. You know how

96

the Yanks are, they want action right away. They can't get used to the pace of life over here."

Looney folded his massive hands in front of his face and closed his eyes for a second or two, then opened them and looked at McGarran. "All right. I've been to America a few times myself, and I know they're all in a mad rush over there. I suppose our lad is just a bit impatient with us. I've made a decision to put my faith in him, but you listen to me," he said, wagging a big finger at McGarran. "If my faith proves to be misplaced, it's you who'll suffer, Seamus McGarran. I'll kill you with my bare hands."

McGarran swallowed hard and nodded his head. "I understand, Jim, I understand."

"And as for you. . ." Looney said, pointing his finger at Pete.

Pete reached out and grabbed Looney's wrist, and pulled his hand down hard. He gripped the man's wrist with such force that Looney could not move it. He put his face close to the big man's and said: "Don't ever point your finger at me, do you understand? I came over here to make a difference for this country, to help out. I'm more loyal than some of the people you have working for you, pal. Just tell me what you need me to do, and let me do it, so I can go home and see my family."

He released Looney's hand, and the big man smiled. "Well, I suppose we've worked things out, then," he said, chuckling as if nothing had happened. "It just so happens I do have a job for you, and you can go home when it's done. I'll need you to get out of town fast, as they used to say in your country's Western movies."

"What's the job?" Pete said.

"It's a bit more complicated than what we've asked you to do so far," Looney said. "You've done a stellar job as a messenger, truck driver, repairman and jack-of-all-trades. You've come in handy more than once when we've needed someone who can use their fists. Now I need your help with something we've been planning for awhile. You may have heard we've been selectively attacking Royal Ulster Constabulary bases. We destroyed one in December of '85, and another last August. Bombs, my lad, that's how we do it. In the last one we knocked down the fence around the base with an earthmover, and then set off a bomb. The plan is to keep at it, till we eliminate every one of their cursed bases, or they surrender, whichever comes first."

"I don't understand what you want me to do," Pete said. "You need a driver for the getaway car?"

"No," Looney said. "I need someone who's good with a gun."

CHAPTER THIRTEEN

April 24, 1987

"You've been working too hard," Jack Caldwell said, bursting through the door of the restaurant kitchen just as Rosie was trying to show the new chef how she wanted the special dinner of local fish prepared. "Come on, I want to take you on a picnic."

"Jack, I can't do that now," Rosie said. "You know I can't leave now. I have a lot of things to go over with Philip. Have you met Philip yet? He's our new--"

"Yes, we've met," Jack said. "My God, Rosie, you're so busy you can't even remember that you introduced me to him two days ago. That's definitely a sign that you're overworked and you need a day off. Come on, I have my bike parked outside and I have a basket with sandwiches, snacks, some slices of cake from the German bakery in Lambertville, and some good wine. It's a gorgeous day, the first really warm day of spring. I'm sure Philip can handle things for a few hours, can't you Philip?"

Philip smiled his craggy, gap-toothed smile, ran a hand through his mop of red hair, and said, "Of course. I'm not a novice at this. I trained at some of the best hotels in New York."

"There, you see?" Jack said, grabbing Rosie by the arm. "He's a seasoned pro, and he doesn't need you looking over his shoulder. Now, come on, and let's take a break for once, dammit."

He wrapped his arms around Rosie and frog walked her toward the door.

"Jack, stop it," Rosie said, trying to wrest free of him. "You know it's the Shad Festival this weekend, and this town will be packed with people. I have to get the restaurant ready for the crowds. Philip is new, and this is his first Shad Fest. I have to get him trained."

"It can wait," Jack said, moving her through the door. "The world isn't going to end if you take a couple hours off this afternoon."

Rosie knew it was futile to resist. One thing she'd learned about Jack Caldwell in these last eight years was that he was a man who didn't take no for an answer. He was impatient with the pace of time, which probably made sense that he was a futurist. He didn't want to wait for things; he wanted them right away.

They walked through the restaurant, which was decorated with pictures of the shad, a local fish that had a history going back to when Native Americans caught it during its annual spring spawning run in the Delaware River. These days the towns of Lambertville and New Hope had made the shad run a tourist draw, and people came from miles around to eat the savory white meat of the fish.

Jack marched her straight outside to the curb, where he had his big black Harley Davidson motorcycle parked.

"Jack, listen, I know this is a sweet idea, but I really don't have--"

"Not another word," Jack said, putting his finger on her lip. "I am here to take you away, to waylay you and get you out of that cavern of a restaurant, and into the sunshine for a few hours." He handed her a red motorcycle helmet, and she sighed and put it on.

Jack put his own blue helmet on, climbed on the front, and she climbed on the back. He kicked the bike's ignition pedal, making it roar into life, and as Rosie put her arms around his lean, muscled waist they took off, and headed over the bridge to Lambertville, New Jersey.

They passed through the small town of Lambertville and then drove north along the Delaware River, and Rosie finally relaxed and just let herself enjoy the beautiful sunshine, the brilliant green leaves on the trees on the hills to her right, and the crisp tang of Spring in the air.

She loved her life here, loved the restaurant and the bar and being part of a community of artistic, vibrant people in New Hope, but sometimes she let herself get too caught up in things, she lost perspective on what was important. It was a relic of her past life, when she jumped into things without thinking, and suffered the consequences as a result.

She was older now, and should have been wiser. She did make better decisions, and in fact she'd been a little too cautious, settling into a rut working for the Dittybopper and his oldies business, when Jack Caldwell had come along and upset her apple cart.

She clutched him closer, feeling the muscles of his back against her, and she was happy once again that she'd met him.

My God, she thought, if I hadn't stopped to talk to him that day on the porch of the hotel, in 1979, if I had just walked on by, I'd still be stuck in that rut. The Dittybopper had a thriving oldies business now, with a radio show and an oldies record store, and a club in New Jersey, but she would have been just an assistant to him, like always, never anything more. He was a fun guy to work for but he was still stuck in a 1950s mindset. He never saw women as equals. There were only four categories of women, for him: singers, fans, girlfriends, or secretaries, and that was it.

She had grown so much in the last eight years, and all because of Jack Caldwell's encouragement. He was always looking for new adventures, always trying to squeeze every ounce of enjoyment out of life, and he never wanted to get stuck in a rut. Rosie still thought he didn't value the past enough, that he was too focused on the future, but their differences added spice to their relationship.

After half an hour of riding north, Jack pulled onto a road that led up the side of a mountain, and Rosie knew where they were going. It was a little bluff that overlooked the river, a lookout point where you could see for miles. It was part of a small park, and Jack liked to go there and commune with Nature.

He pulled the bike into a dirt parking lot that had some picnic tables nearby, and he shut off the engine and listened as the echo of the engine's throb faded into silence. He took off his helmet after a moment, and Rosie doffed hers, and then he helped her off the bike.

"Come on," he said. "It's a perfect afternoon, and we're going to enjoy it."

Rosie knew where he was going. There was a majestic oak tree about 50 yards away that commanded a sweeping view of the river, and Jack loved it. It had a flat area in front of it that was like a wide ledge, and they had come there before and spent time enjoying the view.

He unfastened the brown saddlebags from the bike, then took her hand in his and they walked over. Like always, Rosie was enraptured by the scene in front of her. The Delaware River was wide and full at this point, the current moving along at a strong rate. You could see for miles, and the sun reflecting off the infinite shades of green leaves on the hillside made the river seem like it had a green glow to it. The air had the urgency of spring about it, and the birds and squirrels seemed filled with ecstasy, moving about in a frenzy of exhilaration. Across the river there were herds of deer foraging in the woods, and Rosie thrilled to see their grace and beauty, their movements reminding her of ballet dancers.

"This is beautiful, I have to admit," she said, as they sat on the grass and Jack unpacked the food and wine. "You always pick the right times to do this. I needed to get away. Things have been getting too hectic. Maybe I'm too old to run this operation."

"Nonsense," Jack said. "We are never too old for anything, my dear, you know that's what I believe."

He uncorked a bottle of California pinot noir, poured a glass and gave it to her, then poured one for himself, and held it up for a toast. "Cent'anni!"

It was a favorite toast of his, and it always made Rosie giggle. She drank the wine, then said, "You are such a dreamer, Jack. Sometimes I think you truly believe you'll live to be 100."

"I do!" he said, taking another drink. "I most certainly do. These next 40 years are going to see some of the most rapid cultural change the world has ever known, Rosie. I've said that before, and I believe it. There are world-changing technologies coming, and I want to be around to see them. I believe we'll find a cure for cancer, and most other diseases, our lives will become safer and more pleasant, and we'll all be smarter, better people. We'll be connected in a global network that will be unlike anything the world has ever seen. All we have to do is stay healthy enough to last until they get here." He brought out an assortment of cheeses, all wrapped in tinfoil, and unwrapped them and put them on a plate, then offered it to Rosie.

"I don't know if longevity means enough to me that I'd want to run marathons and become a vegetarian, like you," Rosie said. "If that's what it takes to live to be 100, I might not make it."

"Oh, come on, Rosie," he said. "You have to stick around with me. It won't be any fun without you there. It's going to be a great time to be alive." He pulled a bunch of red grapes out of the bag and gave a handful to Rosie.

Rosie popped several grapes in her mouth and said, "People have always thought the future was going to bring some kind of magical improvement in the world. It's nothing new. Your predictions could be wrong, Jack."

He grinned. "I have a pretty good track record, Rosie. Haven't I steered you right about my stock picks? You've been able to build that bar into a real nice place with the profits you've made from the computer stock I advised you on. And this Microsoft company that I told you to buy last year when they went public, that's the best one yet. You're going to make a lot of money on that one."

Rosie sighed. "I have to admit, you have an uncanny ability to pick stocks. You sure you're not psychic?"

"Nah, I'm not into that stuff," he said. "That's your department. By the way, what's happening in that area? Have you had any more dreams about Pete?"

Rosie's face clouded over. "As a matter of fact, I have. I had one last night. It was all mixed up with my Irish grandmother, and some musicians I can never find, and a lot of bad feelings. I feel he's in danger, Jack, and I'm worried."

Jack stared out at the wide river. "I have to admit, your feelings turn out right almost as much as my stock picks. Have you called him?"

"He's away again. I called the house a few days ago and I got his wife, Betty. She sounds distraught. She said he's been away almost a month this time. It's something to do with Ireland. Betty doesn't know much, but she thinks he's mixed up with the Troubles in the north of Ireland. He's been hanging around some Irish bar in Philly and Betty says she doesn't like the characters he's spending time with. He won't tell her anything, but he seems nervous and angry all the time now, and he leaves on these trips that are getting longer all the time. She's found receipts from pubs in Belfast in his pockets."

"Those people are crazy over there," Jack said. "That's not a good business to be sticking your nose into."

"It's all my fault," Rosie said, taking another drink of wine. "I left him when he was a teenager. I spent nine years in London, and he never forgave me for that. I screwed up his head, and he's got a lot of anger."

Jack looked out at the wide river, taking in the beauty once more. "Didn't you tell me his father was a Brit, and he had a job in the Secret Service or some agency like that over there?"

Rosie laughed. "He did some kind of secret work, yes, but he's been retired for years."

"Maybe he has some connections that could be useful," Jack said. "You could call him."

Rosie thought about it, sipping her wine. "I don't know. I haven't talked to him in years. "Didn't you say he helped you once, when Pete was in 'Nam?" Jack asked

"That was a long time ago, Jack. James Charlesworth is in his late 60s now. He's been retired for years. How much help could he be now?"

Jack shrugged. "It's worth a try, Rosie. Maybe he could find a way to get Pete out of there."

"I don't know. He doesn't represent a good chapter in my life. I don't want to reopen it."

"Suit yourself. But you know I'm just concerned for you, Rosie. I know these problems with Pete are eating you up inside. I don't like to see you like this."

He moved closer to her, putting his arm around her shoulder. Rosie melted into him, and let his strong arms surround her. She was happy to lean on him; things had been wearing her down lately, and she longed to just put her burden aside for a while.

In a moment he was kissing her, and she let herself be swept away by the feel of his sweet lips on hers. He was a masterful kisser, and each time he kissed her was as delicious as the first time he did it, in the empty dining room of the hotel eight years ago when they were in the middle of renovating it. He was replacing a floorboard, and had been sanding it and the air was filled with the smell of wood shavings. Rosie had a paintbrush in her hand and was on the other end of the room painting a window. There was a song playing on the little radio she'd brought, "Only You," by the Platters. All of a sudden Jack had stopped working and walked over to her, taken her in his arms and kissed her full on the lips.

It was like their lips were made for this, like she'd been born to kiss this man, and now she'd found him. Now this time was like all the others. He took his time, moving from her lips to the small of her neck, his lips igniting little fires on her skin, his long fingers running through her hair. He brought his lips back to her mouth, and his tongue found its way inside her mouth, exploring, teasing, playing it like a musical instrument. She ran her fingernails along his neck, in the way that she knew he liked.

They knew each other's bodies very well by now, and they took their time, wanting to make the pleasure last. It was like musicians playing a classic song, lingering over each note, adding little frills and flourishes just to keep it fresh, finding new avenues of pleasure in old familiar melodies. Their skin thrilled to the touch of the other's skin, their breathing matched breath for breath, their fingers trod well-remembered paths to a slow building ecstasy, the familiar vistas of joy.

They knew this spot was secluded, and they had never seen anyone come by in their previous visits. The massive oak tree shielded them from the parking lot, and there was no one on the hill below them. In time they had removed their clothes and cuddled under one of the blankets that Jack had brought, and their bodies melded together like two pieces of a puzzle that fit together with a satisfying click.

He was the completion of her, she knew. Her body, mind, and soul had been made to fit together with this complex, sensitive, masterful man. She could cast off her outward shell and reveal her true self to him, and he to her.

And yet, she had a part of her that held back, even now. Even in the midst of ecstasy, in the height of passion, when she called out his name with manic joy, she knew there was a part held back. Why? What was this hesitation inside her? There was still some part of her that didn't trust, that expected to be disappointed, that was protecting itself from betrayal. Perhaps it was the betrayal of James Charlesworth, all those years ago, that was still haunting her. She had loved him with her whole being, holding nothing back, and it had not been enough. He had told her, on that sunny afternoon by the river, that he was going back to his wife in England. Her innocence had ended that day, and there was a part of her that had never learned to love again.

So, even now, as she moaned with passion and gave herself to Jack, as she felt the fiery presence of his manhood inside her, the selfless giving of himself and the love flowing from inside him, she could not give all. She held back that small, hard, cold place inside, that place with a shell that refused to be opened.

Afterward, with the April breeze wafting through the trees and caressing their faces, she relaxed into his embrace, wanting time to stop so that she could feel this deep serenity forever.

After an hour of simply lying in each other's arms, dozing, they woke up to the sound of people walking along the path below them by the river.

"We'd better get dressed," Jack said. "Before those people come up the hill and get the shock of their lives."

"It won't be a shock for them to see you," Rosie said, scurrying to put her clothes on under the blanket. "You're in fabulous shape for a man your age. I'd be a different matter, though. If they see me naked they'll get quite a fright."

"Well, they can't blame us," Jack said, smirking. "After all, it is spring, when a young man's thoughts turn to sex in the woods."

"Very funny," Rosie said. "Now, hurry up and get dressed. I have to get back to the hotel. I'm too busy to waste any more time up here with you."

"I don't consider this a waste of time," Jack said, sitting up and pulling a t-shirt over his head. "In fact, I think it's the most important thing you'll do all day."

"You have a pretty high opinion of yourself, mister," Rosie said. She had finished dressing, and was rolling up the blanket and gathering the leftover food and wine bottle. "That's not what I meant," Jack said. "Listen, Rosie, there's something I want to say to you."

"I told you, I have to get back," she said. She was going to make a smart remark, but the look on his face made her stop.

"What I meant about this being the most important thing you'll do," he said, taking both of her hands in his, "Is that I want to ask you to marry me." He squeezed her hands and smiled. "I love you, Rosie, and I've known that for a long time now. I never really believed in marriage, but I've come to the opinion that there's nobody I want to spend my life with more than you, and I'm willing to stand in front of a priest, or judge, or Buddhist monk or whatever, and declare that to the world." He got down on one knee and looked up at her, and Rosie could see he was baring his soul to her.

"Will you marry me?"

Rosie felt the world swimming before her eyes. Marriage? It had not been a word she was ever willing to consider. Marriage was something she was planning to do with James Charlesworth, many years ago, but when that didn't happen she just crossed it out of her life. She would have love affairs, yes, but marriage, that concept was out of her life forever. It was not her path, not Rosie Morley, to get married. It was for other people, not her. After all, she came from a line of unhappy marriages. Her father had cheated on her mother and although they had stayed married the fracture was never really healed. Her grandfather, for God's sake, had left her grandmother and married someone else without ever getting a divorce. Men didn't stay true; that was the message she'd learned.

"Rosie?" He was still on one knee, looking up at her with questions in his eyes.

"I, I don't know what to say," she stammered. "I wasn't expecting this. I thought we had a good thing going. No pressure, no commitment. Just having fun, you know."

"I know, but it's different now. I've never met anyone like you, Rosie. I'm ready for this. What do you say?"

She choked back a sob. "I don't know, Jack. I wish you hadn't done this. I just don't, I'm not sure. I do love you, it's not that, but I don't. . . I don't know."

His face fell, and he looked away. "Okay, I guess I can accept that. I guess I wasn't expecting. . . " his voice trailed off.

She got down on her knees and took his face in her hands. "Oh, Jack, I don't want to hurt you. I am so grateful for this." Now the tears were streaming down her face. "Do you know, this is the first time anyone's ever asked to marry me? God, I'm 60 years old, and this is the first time. What a catch I am, huh? I am grateful for this, and I know I should be happy, and I am happy, Jack, it's not that. . . I just, I never thought it would happen. I think I'm still a bit mistrustful of marriage, maybe. I don't know, I'm just so mixed up, like a mixed up teenager I guess. I don't know why you'd want to throw your lot in with somebody like me. Can I think about it? Just give me some time, okay?"

His face lit up, and his natural optimism came back. "Of course," he said, taking her hands in his once again. "Of course. Take as much time as you need. I don't want to rush you. We have all the time in the world, you know. I told you before, I'm going to live to be 100, and I expect you to also."

She laughed, and they stood up. "Well, in that case I think I'll take another eight years to think this over. Maybe by then I'll be able to make up my mind."

"Well, if that's how much time you need," he said, chuckling, "I guess I'll have to live with it. Now, let's get going, since you're in such a hurry to get back."

On the way back, Rosie held on to Jack's waist and leaned her head on his shoulder, feeling so happy and yet so conflicted at the same time.

You're a fool, Rosie, she told herself. You have everything you ever wanted right here, and you should grab it right now, don't let it slip away. Maybe life can turn out good, after all. Maybe there is such a thing as true love, and you can have happiness, true happiness, if you want it.

It was the happiest she'd felt since the times she'd spent with James Charlesworth all those years ago.

And then, when Jack pulled the motorcycle up to the hotel and cut the engine off, she saw Pete's wife Betty sitting on the porch, and she knew her happiness was about to end.

CHAPTER FOURTEEN

Rosie knew immediately that Pete was in danger. It wasn't just the worried look on Betty's face, the circles under her eyes that indicated sleepless nights, or the way she was tapping her foot rapidly as Rosie walked up the steps to greet her. There was a feeling in Rosie's gut, one of those psychic feelings she'd had all her life, that told her with utter certainty that something was wrong.

"Betty, what's the matter?" Rosie said, giving the other woman a hug. "Did something happen to Pete?"

Betty hugged Rosie back, but she was trembling, and she held onto Rosie for long seconds, as if she was a drowning person holding on to a life preserver.

She seemed unable to speak, and Rosie said, "Here, sit down and I'll get you something to drink." She sat Betty at a table on the porch, and Rosie added, "Just stay there a minute. I'll be right back with a glass of wine."

She knew Betty liked Chardonnay, and she went straight back to the bar, found a bottle of Chardonnay, uncorked it and poured two glasses. She took them back to Betty, who seemed to have regained a modicum of control.

They sipped their wine for a moment, and Rosie put her hand on Betty's wrist. "Now, tell me what's wrong. Is it Pete?"

Betty sighed, and her eyes filled with tears. "I think he's in some trouble."

Rosie's heart jumped. Betty had called her before about Pete's strange disappearances, how he was mixed up with some supporters of Northern Ireland's independence, and how he seemed to be getting increasingly angry and preoccupied. Rosie worried about him, but she hadn't spoken to him in several years at this point.

He couldn't seem to let go of the past, and kept blaming her for leaving him in the 1960s. It had all boiled over one Thanksgiving at Pete's house, when he'd told Rosie she was a failure as a mother. That had done it for her. She stormed out of the house, and she hadn't talked to Pete since. If he wanted to carry a grudge, she was prepared to carry it on her side also. She talked to Betty on the phone sometimes, but she hadn't seen Betty or the children in almost a year.

"What happened?" Rosie asked.

"He went away again," Betty said. "And this time, he's been away longer than before. It's been almost a month, and I don't know when he's coming back. I think he's mixed up in something really bad this time, and I'm scared for him."

"Is he in Ireland?"

"Yes," Betty said. "I don't know where, exactly, but I'm sure he's there. He's called me a few times, from phones in pubs, sometimes from a pay phone on the street somewhere. He talks in code. The phone calls are always short, and I get the idea that someone is with him all the time, so he can't say much."

"That's a bad place to be. I see stories on the news all the time about bombings and shootings over there. Is he involved in that?"

Betty's beautiful caramel skin seemed to go pale when Rosie mentioned the violence in Northern Ireland. "He won't tell me what he's doing, except to say he's helping his people throw off the yoke of oppression, all those bullshit political phrases. I keep telling him if he's so fired up about injustice in the world he should come back here. There's plenty of injustice here to fight, and you don't have do it with a gun. That's why we have a legal system." She took a sip of her wine, and the frustration and anger was showing in her trembling hands.

"He's got a lot of anger in him," Rosie said. "I'm to blame for that."

"No," Betty said, sharply. "I don't accept that. We could all spend our whole lives nursing grievances against bad things that happened to us in our childhood. You don't think I wasn't hurt growing up? I'm 40 years old, Rosie. I grew up in the 1950s in Philly, when there were segregated schools, neighborhoods, restaurants. Oh, it wasn't out in the open -- nobody talked about it, except you knew as a black person you weren't welcome in certain places. My brother got beat up so badly he had to go to the hospital after he took a shortcut through an Italian neighborhood once. I can't tell you how many times I had carloads of boys call me names when I was walking to school, or how many times I had teachers tell me in high school I would never get into law school, so I'd better give up my dream of being a lawyer. You don't think I ever fantasized about picking up a gun and shooting one of those bastards? But I didn't, because I believe in working through the system to effect change. Violence only makes things worse. I don't know why Pete doesn't understand that."

"He's a stubborn person," Rosie said. "He was always that way. He gets an idea in his head and he can't shake it."

115

"Don't I know it," Betty said, rolling her eyes. "But there must be something we can do. I need your help, Rosie." Her eyes filled with tears again. "I think he's in a lot of danger this time. I got a phone call from him at 3 AM this morning. He must have snuck away for a few minutes; he was calling from a pay phone. He told me there's something big in the works, another bombing, and they have him working on it. He wouldn't give me too many details, but he sounded scared."

"A bombing? Does he know how to make bombs?"

"Not that I know of, but maybe they've trained him. Or maybe he's just along for the ride, to give them some extra security. He's pretty good with a gun, you know."

"What else did he say?"

"That was it. He hung up fast, because somebody was coming and he said he had to leave. The last thing he said was, 'I love you.'"

Now the tears were coming down her face, and she grabbed Rosie's hand and said, "You have to help me, Rosie. He's in trouble and I don't know what to do."

Rosie pulled her hand away. "He wouldn't accept help from me, Betty. Besides, I don't know what I could possibly do."

"I was thinking his father could help," Betty said. "His father is an English guy, right? You told me once that he worked in the British Navy or something, and had an upper level job. Can you get in touch with him? Maybe he can do something."

Rosie recoiled. "James Charlesworth? But I haven't talked to him in ages. We didn't end on good terms. Plus, I don't even know where he lives. I have an old phone number, but I don't know if it works. No, that's not a solution. Besides, like I said, Pete won't want me getting involved. You know how he feels about me."

"Rosie," Betty said, fixing her eyes directly on her. "I have nowhere else to turn. This is my husband, and your son, and he's in danger. Please. I need you to try."

"He hates me," Rosie said. "You remember what he said about me. He hurt me deeply, and I'm not ready to forgive him."

"You're his mother!" Betty said, slamming her hand on the table so hard it rattled the dishes. "I don't care what he said to you, you can't act that way. He's your son and he's in trouble. What's the matter with you? You can't let a grudge get in the way of your son's life."

Rosie was silent, staring her down.

"Okay," Betty said, pushing her chair back and standing up. "I see I made a mistake coming here. I thought you'd want to help, but clearly you don't. I'll be seeing you, Rosie."

She turned to go, but Rosie reached out and grabbed her wrist.

"Okay," Rosie said. "Maybe I can finally do something right for Pete. I'll call Charlesworth."

CHAPTER FIFTEEN

May 6, 1987

"You're a bit nervous, aren't you, Yank?" Con Wilson said. "Why don't you relax and play cards with the rest of us?"

"I don't want to play cards," Pete said. He was standing in the kitchen of a little house at the end of a winding lane in County Armagh, a safe house where Jim Looney had six of his best men holed up, in preparation for tomorrow's attack on the nearby RUC base at Loughgall. There were six other men in another house in the area, and Looney was meeting with them at present. He was to arrive in an hour or so to brief Con Wilson's team about the plans.

"Why not?" Wilson said. "Cards are a good way to occupy your mind before an operation like tomorrow. It keeps you from thinking too much, perhaps losing your nerve. "It was a pointed remark, like so many of Wilson's comments directed at Pete.

"Don't worry about me," Pete sneered. "I don't lose my nerve." He was edgy, and he kept pacing around the kitchen, with occasional forays out to the back yard. He wouldn't admit it to Con Wilson, but the very idea of playing cards made him go cold inside. In Vietnam everybody played cards before a big battle. Guys would make outrageous bets, brag, talk about all the enemy soldiers they were going to kill the next day. Pete couldn't stand looking at cards now, because it reminded him of all the guys who weren't there for the next card game.

For the dozenth time Pete went out the back door and paced around the grounds. Up above him the moon was peeking through scattered clouds, and he thought again of his family at home. It was

9:00 at night here, which meant it was 3:00 in Philadelphia, right around the time school let out. His daughter Rosalie was probably getting on the school bus to come home. When the bus dropped her off at the corner she would come racing up the steps and burst through the door and ask if Daddy was home. Her grandmother, Betty's mother, who helped out with the babysitting while Betty was at work, would have to tell her Pete wasn't there.

He clasped his hands in front of him in prayer. He was not a religious man, but he had a feeling that there was something up there he should pray to at a time like this.

"I don't know how to say this," he prayed silently, "but I need some help here. I have a bad feeling about what I'm mixed up in. These guys seem like a bunch of bumblers who are going to screw things up royally tomorrow night. I have no faith in them at all, but I'm trapped here with them. And, hell, even if I thought they were a bunch of experts at this kind of operation, I have no heart for it anymore. I'm sick of fighting; all it does is make things worse. Nobody is ever truly beaten unless they're dead, and even then the anger lives on to cause more pain and suffering. It's an endless cycle. It's been going on in this country for centuries, and it never really changes. Those guys in there will think they've won if they blow up another barracks tomorrow, but all they will have done is add more fuel to the fire that's raging through this country.

"I want to see my family again, God," he prayed. "I've been a lousy, stubborn father and I took my eye off what was important. My wife, my kids, I should be with them. I swore I wasn't going to abandon my kids like my mother did to me, but it looks like I did just that. Now I might never get back to them if something goes wrong tomorrow. Please, God, get me out of this mess. I'll be a better husband and father, and yes, I'll be a better son to my mother.

I just need to get out of this place. I don't want to shoot anybody, and I sure don't want to get shot, or blown up."

He looked up at the sky. The moon had disappeared behind a bank of clouds, and the night was pitch black now. His heart sunk. He felt like his prayers weren't going to be answered, and a yawning despair took hold of him. For the umpteenth time he thought of running away, but he knew that would not work. Larry Flynn knew exactly where Betty and the children lived, and he would exact retribution, just as he said he would. There was no way out; he was trapped.

He heard the laughter and shouts of the men in the kitchen, and he shook his head. They were all just as scared as him, he knew that. Everyone is a coward the night before a battle. Men tried to hide their fear with a show of bravado, but inside they were shaking. He'd better go back, or they'd start to wonder where he was. He moved toward the back porch, then all of a sudden he saw the headlights of a car coming up the dirt road toward the house. He waited on the back porch and in a moment the car pulled up, and Jim Looney got out.

"What are you doing out here?" he said. "Having a smoke to calm your nerves?"

"I don't smoke," Pete said. "And I told you before, I don't get nervous in situations like this."

"That's good, lad," Looney said, walking up on the porch. "I'll need your steely calm tomorrow. Now come inside with me, I have some things to go over with the rest of the lads."

Inside, Looney sat down at the kitchen table, and after taking a drink from a bottle of whiskey that was being passed around, he went to the sink and poured it down the drain.

"Jim, that's good whiskey you're wasting," one of the men said.

"I don't care," Looney said, with a snarl. "I told you blockheads not to drink the night before, and what do I find, but a bottle of this stuff being passed around? I want clear heads tomorrow, and if I catch anyone else taking a drop between now and when we head out to do the job, I'll cut your tongue out. Do you hear me?" he roared.

"Yes," they all muttered.

"Now, let's go over the plan one more time," he said, sitting down at the table again.

For the next hour Looney went over every detail, making the men repeat what he said at critical points. There were two teams involved in this operation, and they were going to meet up tomorrow evening at 7, where they'd attack the RUC base. One team would go at 6:00 to a farm two miles west of Loughgall. They were to drive to the farmhouse, tie up the farmer and his family, and steal the digger, or backhoe loader that the farmer had in his garage. McGarran was to drive the digger the two miles to the location of the RUC base, with two men driving in front of him in a scout car, to make sure no police stopped the digger. When McGarran reached the RUC base he was to drive the big machine right through the fence, leaving a gaping hole for the other team, which would rendezvous with them in a stolen van, to drive through. Then they'd all jump out and start firing their weapons at every RUC man they could find.

"Now, we'll need two men to stay at the farmhouse, to keep things quiet there," Looney said. "I want O'Rourke to go, and you, Morley."

"What?" Con Wilson said, incredulous. "Why are you leaving the Yank behind? I thought he was part of this operation."

"He is," Looney said. "I need a cool head at the farmhouse. He and O'Rourke can stay there till we come back for them."

Pete looked at O'Rourke, who was a ruddy-faced Australian with a mashed up nose and scars on his face from brawling. He was not very smart, and he screwed his face up with the effort of processing what Looney had just said.

Con Wilson didn't like it. "So the Yank is to get a pass on the fighting, is he?" Wilson said. "I bet that sits well with you, Yank, doesn't it? You don't have to get your hands dirty. No chance for you to back up all your talk about Vietnam now."

"I don't need to prove anything to you," Pete said. "But if you want me to back up my words, I'm happy to go outside and settle things now." He was gripping the table hard, and he could easily have lunged across it and attacked Wilson.

"That's enough," Looney roared. "I'm running this operation, Con Wilson, not you. I want the Yank at the farmhouse, and that's the end of it. If you need to know the reason, it's because he's not a local. You know as well as I that this is a small country and everybody is related somehow, or they know your second cousin or your neighbor down the road. The Yank is an outsider, and O'Rourke's lived in Australia for 15 years, so nobody knows him either. They're going to be cooped up with that farmer for a couple of hours, plenty of time for the stupid sod to ask a lot of questions. If

122

I send one of you apes there he'll find some way to identify you later on, but O'Rourke and the Yank will be strangers to him.

"I understand, Jim," Wilson said, "But, really, don't you think--"

"That's enough!" Looney roared, banging the table so hard with his fist that it rattled the plates and glasses. "One more word out of you, boyo, and you'll be picking your teeth off the floor. Now shut up and just do your job tomorrow, and don't be worrying about anyone else."

Wilson seemed ready to snarl a reply, but thought better of it. He gave Pete a menacing look, and Pete stared him down.

Pete had no idea why Looney wanted him to stay at the farmhouse, but he was immensely relieved. It meant he probably would not have to fire a gun tomorrow, and that was a pleasant prospect. He couldn't believe his luck -- maybe he'd get out of this situation without hurting someone, or being hurt himself. Or ending up in prison.

He wondered if his prayers had been answered, but whatever the case, he couldn't believe his good fortune.

That night he lay in a creaky, narrow bed with springs poking through the mattress into his back, but he didn't mind the discomfort at all. He stared out the window in the bedroom where he was sleeping with three other men who were snoring loudly, and he saw the moon's light refracted by the branches of a tree, and felt a peace he hadn't felt for years. There was no fight in him any longer, and he knew he was going to get his fervent wish to go home to his family.

Thank you, Lord, he prayed silently. I know it's you that did this, somehow. Maybe my old Irish grandmother had a hand in it, too.

He had been almost 14 when his grandmother Rose died, and he remembered visiting her in the home where she lived out her last years. She had snow white hair and piercing green eyes, and there were times when she'd talk or sing songs in Gaelic, the words sounding guttural and harsh to Pete's ears. She had a kindly smile, though, especially when Pete was around, and he remembered how devoted she was to the Blessed Virgin. He remembered his mother saying that the old woman died in church, praying to the Virgin.

Maybe she's helping me, he thought. After all, this is the country where she was born, and where her ancestors came from. It's probably riddled with the ghosts and spirits of my ancestors. I thank you, grandmother, for whatever help you're giving me, he thought.

CHAPTER SIXTEEN

The next day passed slowly, as the men waited anxiously for the operation to start. Pete stayed away from Con Wilson, not wanting to provoke the other man into doing something violent. There was no sense in getting hurt now, when he was so close to getting out of here.

Toward evening Looney came by and gave them their final instructions. He distributed black woolen ski masks to all of them, and said, "Don't take them off under any circumstances. I don't want anyone getting a look at you."

They put their ski masks on and he took them out to the car, a boxy little red Citroen, and all of them crowded into it. Con Wilson sat in the front passenger seat, so Pete squeezed into the back with two other men. Looney drove them several miles down winding country roads, passing herds of black and white cows and the occasional tractor, and then they made a sharp turn and went up a hill to a farmhouse of whitewashed stone with a dilapidated gray barn next to it, where Pete could see the orange digger parked.

"Now, make it fast, lads," Looney said. "His name is Macaleer, and he's inside eating his supper with the missus. Get in there and tie him up pronto!"

The men barreled out of the car and straight in the front door, while Pete and O'Rourke went around back in case the farmer tried to make a quick escape. Pete could hear loud voices inside, and the screams of the farmer's wife. There was a slapping sound, and then she stopped screaming, although you could hear a quiet sobbing after that. Then there was Looney's voice, shouting: "Now, just give us the keys to that big orange machine out there, and nobody gets hurt. Do you understand, mate? Where are the keys?"

The farmer must have done what he asked, because the next thing Pete knew Looney and McGarran came out the back door and made their way to the barn. McGarran jumped into the seat of the digger, put the key in the ignition, and the machine roared to life, shaking like a steam engine.

"All right, let's get to it," Looney barked. "O'Rourke and the Yank, you get inside and make sure Mr. Macaleer and his wife don't cause us any trouble. McGarran, you start this infernal machine down the road to Loughgall, and the rest of you get in the car with me. We're going to go ahead of McGarran and make sure everything goes smoothly."

The men piled into Looney's car and it took off down the road, while McGarran put his machine into gear and followed at a slower pace. Pete and O'Rourke went inside the farmhouse, where they found the farmer and his wife tied to chairs in the kitchen.

They were terrified, of course. Their mouths were stuffed with bandanas, but their eyes were as big as saucers, and they were shaking. They clearly thought they were going to be shot, and Pete felt sorry for them.

He walked over to the farmer's wife, a plump woman in a faded green dress and a woolen shawl, and pulled the gag out of her mouth.

"Thank you," she said, exhaling loudly.

"What are you doing?" O'Rourke said.

126

"There's no need for this," Pete said, walking over to the farmer and pulling the gag out of his mouth. "They looked like they were suffocating."

"You blokes will never get away with this," Macaleer said, his face blotchy red with anger. "They'll catch every last one of you and send you to prison."

"Shut up, you Protty dog, or I'll brain you," O'Rourke said. He was carrying a pistol, and he held the butt of it up as if he were going to smack Macaleer in the head with it.

"Ian, keep your mouth shut," his wife said. "Please, these are desperate men. Don't provoke them."

"They're a bunch of IRA trash, and I spit on them," Macaleer said, spitting at O'Rourke's feet.

The Australian lashed out with his gun, hitting the farmer across the cheek with it, and there was a sound of metal against bone. The blow opened a gash on the farmer's cheek, and his wife screamed in anguish.

"Stop it!" Pete said. "You don't need to hurt him."

"I won't have this stupid farmer spitting on my shoes," O'Rourke snarled. "He's nothing but a Loyalist shit, and I'll kill him if he does it again."

"Just calm down," Pete said. The farmer's wife was sobbing in her chair, but Macaleer was glaring at O'Rourke as if he wanted to spit at him again.

"Why don't you go turn on the TV in the other room," Pete said. "There must be a good soccer match on, or football, or whatever you call it over here."

That seemed to tickle O'Rourke's fancy, for he grinned and said, "I don't mind if I do. And I'll help meself to a bottle of this bastard's whiskey, too. Let's see what we have in here," he said, walking over to a cabinet by the refrigerator and opening it. He found a bottle of whiskey inside, smiling as he held it up to read the label.

"Oh, this is the good stuff," he said, grinning behind his ski mask. "Jamison's. You have good taste, for a Protty dog." He unscrewed the cap, tilted the bottle back and took a long swig of the whiskey. When he was finished he wiped the back of his hand across his mouth, then said, "Cheerio, Mate," and headed out to the living room to turn on the TV.

Pete stood there with the farmer glaring at him and the man's wife sobbing silently in her chair. He wanted to tell them not to worry, that everything would be all right, but he didn't want to appear soft in front of O'Rourke.

He also thought it was probably not a good idea to talk to them, since he didn't want to be identified by his American accent. All he wanted now was for this operation to go off smoothly, and for Looney to come back and get him, so he could catch a plane out of Dublin and go home.

He sat down at the kitchen table and picked up a local newspaper and began to read. The clock on the wall ticked loudly, and Macaleer's wife kept whimpering, but otherwise there was nothing to break the silence besides the sound of the TV in the other room. O'Rourke was watching some kind of a comedy, and he was laughing uproariously at various times.

Pete was engrossed in reading a story about the local political situation, with a speech reprinted by the firebrand Unionist preacher Ian Paisley, when all of a sudden there was a hand clamped around his mouth. He breathed in and suddenly everything went blank.

When he came to it was because he had a wave of nausea that felt like his stomach was turning inside out. He couldn't think of anything but vomiting, and his whole body shook with the effort of retching. Within seconds he had spilled his guts onto his lap, and the car (for it appeared he was in a car), came to a screeching halt. He had some kind of hood on his head, and his hands were restrained by handcuffs, but he heard the squeal of brakes, and the car swerved onto what felt like gravel or dirt, and stopped.

"Blimey, he's just honked all over me," a voice said. "Lord, that smells awful."

"Get him out before he does it again," another voice said. "Quick, we don't have much time. Let him empty his guts on the berm."

A car door opened and Pete was shoved outside, walked a few feet down a hill, and then his hood was yanked off his head.

"Where am I?" he said, but before his eyes could focus in the dark, a fist rammed into his stomach, and the nausea welled up again, and he started to fall to his knees. "Hold him, so he doesn't soil himself," a voice said, and someone grabbed him from behind, under the shoulders.

He couldn't hold back; he emptied the contents of his stomach in one long retching wave. He kept going till he had nothing left, but still his body shook with dry heaves. When he finally finished his limbs were trembling and he had a splitting headache.

"Right, get him back in the van," the rough voice said. "Come on, make it quick. We don't have all night, you know."

The man who was holding Pete dragged him back to the van and threw him roughly into a seat, strapped him in, and then the van started off again on the bumpy road. Pete was exhausted from the effort of throwing up, and in minutes he drifted off into unconsciousness again.

He awoke much later on a bed with the sound of a TV playing in the next room. There was a bare light bulb in the ceiling, and the glare of it was hurting his eyes. The headache was back, worse than ever. It felt like a team of carpenters was hammering nails inside his skull. The bed was creaky, and the wallpaper across from it was in a lurid green and yellow zigzag pattern that almost made him retch again. In fact, he suddenly realized he did have to retch once more, and he leaned over the side of the bed and vomited. Luckily someone had placed a steel pot there, and he didn't miss it.

The sound of his vomiting brought voices into the room, and he recognized the voice of the leader from the night before.

"Still feeling badly, are you?" he said. "Sorry for that, old chum, but it happens sometimes with chloroform. Nothing we can do about it." It was an English accent, and Pete looked up and saw a man with a clipped brown mustache and short hair, who carried himself like a military man, although he wasn't wearing a uniform.

"Who are you?" Pete said.

"Oh, that doesn't matter," the man said. "I'm just a chap who's doing a job."

"What do you mean?" Pete said. "What kind of a job? And where am I? Where is O'Rourke?"

"I'll answer your last question first," the man said. "O'Rourke is dead. He didn't want to cooperate when we tried to tell him it was in his best interest to come with us. He became very belligerent and tried to shoot at us. That wasn't a good idea."

"Oh," Pete said.

"And I'll answer the next question, which may be forming in your mind now, which is what happened to your IRA friends who were going to attack that barracks. I'm afraid most of them are dead too."

"Dead?" Pete's brain seemed to be working slowly, and he had a hard time digesting the words the man had just said. "What do you mean, dead?"

"Exactly what I said. They lost the element of surprise, I'm afraid. There was an informer who tipped us off. Our people were waiting for them."

"You bastards," Pete said. He tried to get up, intending to punch the man, whose air of superiority was beginning to grate on him. He rose to his feet but his legs buckled under him, and he fell to the floor. The man lifted him and put him back on the bed.

131

"You'll need to watch that," the man said. "It takes awhile for the legs to work again. Sorry, but that's just a side effect of the drug we use."

"You better get out of here, because as soon as I'm able I'm going to tear you apart," Pete said.

"I'm sorry to hear that," the man said. "I'll chalk up your belligerence to the fact that you're still disoriented. However, I have someone who wants to see you, and he can explain things better. I'll leave you now, and let him visit with you."

He strode out of Pete's field of vision and went out the door. In a moment the door opened again and Pete heard someone walk over to the bed. He looked up to see a man with wavy gray hair in a crisp blue pinstriped suit with a white shirt and a maroon tie looking down at him. He blinked, thinking he'd seen that face before somewhere. "Who are you?" he said.

"I'm James Charlesworth," the man said. "Your father."

CHAPTER SEVENTEEN

Pete sat bolt upright, even though the effort brought back his splitting headache. "Ow," he said, holding his hand up to his forehead. "That hurts."

"I'm sorry," Charlesworth said. "They told me you should be feeling better soon."

"What did you mean, saying you were my father?" Pete said. "I don't have a father."

"I'm afraid you do," Charlesworth said. "Has your mother not told you about me? I know I haven't been a part of your life, but I thought she might have told you."

It was hard to focus his eyes in the bright glare from the light bulb above him, so Pete put his head in his hands for a moment and closed his eyes to rest them.

"She told me my father was an English guy she met during World War II," Pete said, slowly, as if it was an effort to get the words out. "She avoided talking about it. I got angry with her once when I was a teenager and made her tell me. She just said you were a fling she had as a kid, that's all."

"A fling?" Charlesworth said. His voice sounded hurt. "I am sorry that's how she remembers it. I thought it was more than that. I certainly wanted it to be more than that, although I admit I behaved despicably at the time."

"She said you left her and went back to England at the end of the war." Pete was looking at the floor, unable to meet the gaze of the man standing above him.

"That's correct. I had a wife and a child back there. I thought that's where I belonged. I admit I behaved as though my relationship with your mother was indeed a wartime fling. It was a beastly thing to do, leaving her like that. I never forgot her, though. Never. And when she came to London in the 1960s, I--"

"Is that why she came over there?" Pete said, raising his eyes to meet Charlesworth's with a fierce glare. "To be with you? Is that why she stayed so goddam long, leaving me practically an orphan for ten years?"

"No, I'm afraid that wasn't the reason," Charlesworth said. "I ran into her by accident. I was dumbstruck to meet her walking down a street in London. I had never stopped thinking about her, and when I saw her again it was like my heart opened up once more. I was dead inside, Pete, and she gave me life again. Those were some of the happiest years of my life. But it didn't last, I'm sad to say. She told me she wasn't in love with me anymore. She said she had to go home, because she missed you terribly, and she wanted to be with you. I wanted to come with her, but she said no. That was fifteen years ago. I haven't seen or heard from her again. Not until last week."

Pete was puzzled. "A week ago? What do you mean?"

Charlesworth sat down on the bed next to him. "I know this is probably a lot for you to take in, Pete, but Rosie called me to get you out of here. She said your wife came to her and asked for help, because she thought you were in danger."

"My mother called you?" Pete said, still unable to process this information.

"Yes. She was quite worried about you."

"Ha!" Pete sneered. "Funny that she would worry about me now. She didn't seem to worry much when she left me for ten years. She's not much of a mother. She's never been a big part of my life."

Charlesworth sighed. "Don't judge her too harshly. She did the best she could, I'm sure. We all make mistakes. We're all just fumbling around in the dark, trying to find our way."

"I don't want her help," Pete said.

"No, it was good that she called me. These are desperate people you're involved with, Pete, and things were not going to end well for you."

"They're fighting for a good cause," Pete snapped.

"I won't get into the rightness of their cause," Charlesworth said, "but the fact is they've killed a lot of British subjects, and my government is committed to hunting them down. They've chosen violence as their path, and it's caused a lot bloodshed and heartache in this ancient land. You were fated to come to a bad end in that last operation. There was an informer, and our people knew exactly what was going to happen. They were waiting for your friends."

"How do you know all this?"

"I used to work in the government, for a branch of the intelligence service. I'm long retired now, but I still have friends who can make things happen. I called some people and found out what was in the works. They got you out in time, Pete."

Pete massaged his temples, trying to clear his head. "Did you say there was an informer? That can't be right. Those guys are freedom fighters. They believe in their cause. None of them would sell out their brothers. You're wrong about that!"

Charlesworth sighed deeply. "I'm afraid you're mistaken, Pete. One thing I learned in my years of service is that there are always people willing to sell out their cause. It happens all the time. You know Big Jim Looney?"

Pete's mouth dropped open. "You're not saying it was him? Jim Looney? No, that can't be right. He was the leader of the operation. He was the last guy who--"

"The last one you'd expect to sell out his comrades, right?" Charlesworth said, a smile flickering at the edge of his lips. "Those are usually the ones who do it. Looney was playing both sides of the street. He was looking out for himself, Pete, not anything or anyone else. If you read the newspaper reports of the dead in the ambush, you won't see his name among them. He was spared, because of his usefulness."

Pete tried to take it all in. "Looney? I don't know. . . I sure thought he was a true Irish patriot. . . it's hard to believe." Suddenly, he was filled with anger, and he punched the bed. "Damn, I could have gotten killed because of that guy. I put my life in danger. So did everybody else."

"Yes, but thank God your mother called me, and I was able to protect you," Charlesworth said. He put his hand on Pete's arm. "I am glad I got to see you, Pete. I used to wonder what you looked like, how you talked, what you'd be like as an adult. I never thought I'd have the chance to find out. This has been a blessing for an old man like me."

"I used to wonder about you too," Pete said, scowling. "I wanted to know more about you; that's why I asked my mother so many questions. I was angry at you for a long time."

"I don't blame you," Charlesworth said. "I should have been part of your life."

"You could have tried to get in touch," Pete said, his voice rising. "You could have tried."

"I wanted to," Charlesworth said. "I sincerely did. But, as I said, Rosie made it clear she didn't want me in her life at all -- or yours."

"Yeah, I know she can be stubborn," Pete said. "So can I."

"I suppose it runs in the family," Charlesworth said. "But don't let stubbornness cause you to make bad decisions. You need to go home to your family now. If you believe strongly enough in a united Ireland, you can raise money for it, write to your politicians, do whatever you can behind the scenes -- but for God's sake don't get mixed up in the guns and bombings over here. You owe it to your family to stay alive. My friends in the next room will have you on a plane home tomorrow -- I would advise you not to come back."

Pete nodded his head. "I hear you. I'm at the point where I want to go home and live a quiet life. The thing is, there are some people over there who were holding me hostage, forcing me to get involved over here. I owed them some money and this was how they wanted me to pay it back. They said my family would get hurt if I didn't cooperate. They were pretty dangerous guys."

Charlesworth smiled. "My friends in the next room are very capable of handling situations like that. You just tell them the

137

details, and I feel certain that by the time you get off your plane in Philadelphia your problem will be solved."

"But that's in America," Pete said. "Not over here. You guys can't--"

"Tut, tut," Charlesworth said, holding his hand up. "All things are possible, my boy, all things are possible. You just take your plane home and give your wife and children a lot of hugs, and let us worry about everything else."

He stood up. "It's time for me to go. My wife thinks I'm away visiting my old school chums, but I need to get back before too long or she'll start asking questions. I'd rather endure three days' interrogation by the Chinese than submit to her questions for an hour."

He put his hand on Pete's shoulder. "I am glad I got the chance to meet you, Pete. It's been an honor. You're a fine young man. I'm proud of the fact that you're willing to fight for what you believe in. I would have liked to be a bigger part of your life, but it was not to be."

Pete still couldn't stand up, but he put his hand on top of Charlesworth's.

"Thanks," he said. "I'm glad I met you too. And thanks for helping me today."

"It was my pleasure," Charlesworth said. "Give my love to your family. I don't expect I'll see you again, Pete. I'm an old man, and there's not much time ahead of me. Goodbye, son."

He turned to go.

"Wait," Pete said. He reached in his pants pocket, found the brown leather wallet where he carried pictures of his family, and pulled it out. "I want you to see these. Here are your grandchildren."

Charlesworth came back as Pete stood up shakily, and he took the pictures from Pete of the little girl and boy, Rosalie and Marty. He smiled broadly, looking at them. "They're beautiful," he said. "And the girl, she looks exactly like her grandmother Rosie. I bet she's a little spitfire."

"Oh, yes," Pete said. "That's her mother Betty in the picture with her. She's got some of both of us in her."

Charlesworth handed the photos back, with tears in his eyes. "I appreciate this. If there's anything further I can do for you, tell Rosie to get in touch with me. Goodbye, Pete."

"Goodbye, Dad," Pete said.

CHAPTER EIGHTEEN

October, 1988

Rosie made it her business to check on Lorenzo after Mercy died, inviting him to her restaurant for lunch every day. He tried to keep his spirits up, and he kept busy with the bookshop, opening every day and seeming to enjoy his interactions with the customers. It was clear that he missed Mercy, but he was trying his hardest to deal with it.

He was a man in his 80s now, and Rosie worried about what would happen to him. As the years went on he seemed to be working harder to maintain his optimistic attitude. His body seemed to be getting shorter, and he had more white hair with each passing year. His cough came and went, but he stubbornly refused to go to a doctor about it.

Then one day he said, "What ever happened to that idea of Jack's to go visit the house where your grandparents worked? Mercy wanted to see it, and we were all set to go when she died. I just got a shipment of books last week, and there was one about Chestnut Hill. It made me think of that house."

"Really?" Rosie said. "I thought it would be too painful for you. Are you sure?"

"Of course I am," Lorenzo said. "It feels like unfinished business to me, and I want to finish it. Can Jack still arrange a tour for us?"

"I'm sure he can," Rosie said. "I'll talk to him about it."

"Good," Lorenzo said. "Let me know when, and I'll get someone to cover for me at the bookshop. I'll drive, by the way. I love to drive people around. It makes me remember the good times driving my cab."

So it was arranged for the following week, and on the appointed day Lorenzo picked Rosie and Jack up just after the lunchtime rush at the hotel, when Rosie felt secure about leaving the restaurant for a few hours. Rosie sat in the passenger seat of Lorenzo's blue Ford Taurus, and Jack sat behind her. They had been bickering all morning, but Lorenzo seemed relaxed and happy, and his good mood buoyed them.

"I love to drive on days like this," he said, opening the window and sticking his elbow out, looking for all the world like the cabbie he'd been. "The sun is out, there's a gentle breeze, the colors of the world are especially vivid. It's a day when you feel glad to be alive, isn't it?"

"It certainly is, Lorenzo," Rosie said, marveling at this man's ability to see happiness all around him. As Lorenzo drove along the winding roads by the Delaware River, and then through Bucks County, he whistled songs, told jokes, reminisced about some of the interesting people he'd had in his cab. He was a fount of wisdom about local history, too, and expounded on all the artists and writers who'd lived in Bucks County over the years.

"Did you know that Oscar Hammerstein III had a place here?" he said. "He wrote the music for so many of those classic Broadway shows, like Showboat, Music Man, etc. Some of the famous writers from the 1920s, the members of the Algonquin Round Table, they had houses here. Dorothy Parker, S.J. Perelman. Oh, this area was just full of creative people. There was even a school of art, the New Hope School, that flourished here in the late 1800s."

His discourse was interrupted several times by coughing fits, and although Rosie was worried every time it happened, Lorenzo laughed it off. "It's a genetic thing," he said. "My Pop had a cough like this when he got older. It's probably something to do with all the talking I've done in my life. I probably wore out my vocal cords."

As they got closer to the city, Lorenzo gave explanations of various neighborhoods: when the houses were built, what ethnic groups first lived there, what kind of jobs the residents worked at, what famous people were born there, and on and on.

It was after 3:00 when they got to Chestnut Hill, and they could see schools letting out as they passed them. They followed a school bus down a street that ended in a cul-de-sac, and when they stopped, Lorenzo pointed out a massive stone fountain with ornate classical Greek style statues. There was no water flowing in it, but it was impressive nonetheless.

"That used to be part of the Stotesbury estate," he said. "This area, called Wyndmoor, used to be part of a huge estate owned by a man named Edward T. Stotesbury. He was a wealthy banker in the 1920s who built a mansion called Whitemarsh Hall, and it was a real palace. It was designed by Horace Trumbauer, a famous architect, and it was six stories, with three of them underground. It had 147 rooms, 45 bathrooms, and it took up 100,000 square feet. It had a ballroom, a gym, a movie theater, and its own refrigerating plant."

"My God," Jack said, astonished. "All that was here?"

"Yes," Lorenzo said. "It was an amazing estate. It took a staff of forty to run the place. They had fancy balls and parties where dignitaries from other countries came."

The school bus let off some of its passengers, children who ran laughing down the street to their houses, which were modest stone two-story affairs.

"What happened to it?" Rosie said. "It's not here anymore, right?"

"No," Lorenzo said, putting the car in gear and making a left turn to get away from the school bus. "The 1930s weren't kind to Stotesbury. He lost a lot of money in the stock market crash, and then he died suddenly in 1938. His wife couldn't afford the upkeep, and she had to sell the place in the 1940s."

"I never knew there was so much money around here," Rosie said.

"Oh, yes, and it's Old Money," Lorenzo said. He drove along Paper Mill road, then made a turn on to Stenton Avenue, and then onto the cobblestoned streets of Chestnut Hill. "Many of these houses were built a hundred or more years ago. The people who owned them made their money from the railroads, or they were merchants, or bankers. Some of them had families that were here before the Revolutionary War. They're old line WASPS, and a lot of their descendants still live in these houses."

"Living on their trust funds," Jack said. "I hate people like that. They don't innovate, don't bring anything new to the table, they're just living on what their grandfathers did."

143

"You're right," Lorenzo said. "Some of them are stuck in the past. There are a few who try to live useful lives, though. They collect art, start foundations, sit on boards of directors of charitable organizations. They try to contribute.

"Besides, not all of these houses still have the same families living in them," he continued. "They've been sold, cut up, remodeled. The neighborhood is less pretentious than it was 100 years ago. These are just upper middle class folks, for the most part."

He turned down a leafy street with gray brick houses set back from the sidewalk, most of them surrounded by majestic oak and maple trees that looked at least 50 years old. "This is a prime example," he said. "And it looks like this is the house we're looking for, right Jack?"

Jack peered at the number on the black metal mailbox out front. It had 4522 in gold letters. "That's the place," Jack said.

Lorenzo drove up the wide driveway and parked at the side of the house, near an old garage. They got out and surveyed the house. It was a three-story building made of gray stone, and it had two turrets, like a castle, and a copper roof that had gone green with age. It had maroon shutters and a wide porch painted maroon also. There were signs that it had been modernized, but the core of the house probably looked the same as it did 100 years earlier. The lawn was elegantly manicured, but it was dominated by the majestic trees that rose a hundred feet in the air.

Rosie could feel a strange presence, and she shivered. She seemed to hear music at the edge of her hearing. She looked around, but there was no activity on the street. The house seemed full of dignity, full of majesty, full of the many lives that had been lived in it.

"Well, no need to stand here like we're in a church," Jack said, stretching his arms as he got out of the car. "It's a house, not a monument. Let's go introduce ourselves."

He led the way up the wide front steps and to big oak double doors with brass handles and thick, old-fashioned wavy glass panes.

He rang the doorbell, and a woman came to the door. She was a stout, late fiftyish woman who had sandy red hair tied up in a bun, and she was wearing a white linen dress. She smiled warmly, and said, "Come in, come in, my name is Molly Watts. My husband is delayed at school, but he'll be here shortly."

She welcomed them into the spacious foyer, which had a large Oriental rug, a splendid brass chandelier, a large blue and white porcelain vase, and wallpaper in a flowery gold and blue pattern that was pleasing to the eye.

Jack introduced the group, and Molly shook all of their hands. "I understand you're here for a tour, but first let's go in the kitchen and have some tea. I've made a pot of it for you."

She led the way into the kitchen, a large room with a black and white linoleum floor, a large butcher-block table, stainless steel stove, and copper pots hanging from the wall. "I used to work in restaurants," she said, "and I still love to cook, which is why this room is set up like a restaurant kitchen."

She was a sunny, pleasant woman who seemed happy to see them. She sat them down at the butcher-block table and poured mugs of tea for them, and brought out plates of chocolate cookies and a carrot cake that had the creamiest icing Rosie had ever tasted.

"Mmm," she said, taking a bite of the cake. "I'd hire you in a minute to bake cakes at my restaurant in New Hope."

Molly laughed heartily. "Oh, my, I would have jumped at your offer ten years ago, but I'm not really looking for an opportunity like that. I bake for a few restaurants here in Chestnut Hill, but I'm not looking to expand. But, anyway, let's get back to the purpose of your visit. Mr. Caldwell said you had relatives who lived here?"

"Yes," Rosie said. "My grandparents."

"And my deceased wife's father," Lorenzo said.

"And my great uncle and aunt," Jack said, laughing. "As you can see, we're all connected through family members who lived here."

"Isn't that interesting?" Molly said. "Well, this place has been around for a very long time, so I suppose there are a lot of people who've passed through here. I see some of them from time to time."

Rosie put her mug down with a clatter. "You mean you see ghosts?"

Molly smiled. "I prefer to call them spirits. Yes, this house has many of them. They're out and about at various times, in various rooms. We bought it twenty years ago, and the owner at that time was a very proper Episcopalian man who didn't want to talk about it. I'd heard some stories, because I grew up nearby and people talked about strange things happening here, but I think he disapproved. He acted like he'd never seen anything strange here, but I believe he was stonewalling us. Luckily my husband is a History professor, and he has enough respect for the past that he's actually excited that we have spirits here."

"What kind of spirits do you see?" Rosie said. "I mean, who are they?"

"Oh, I think they're people who lived here, obviously," Molly said. "They hang around certain rooms, and you might see a wisp of misty light. Other times you may be walking along a hallway upstairs and you'll suddenly feel a chill draft, like you just opened a refrigerator door. There are times when I hear strange music playing, just at the edge of my hearing. Or a door will close when there's no reason for it to. Things have fallen off tables when there's nobody in the room."

"You've never seen anything, though?" Rosie said. "You haven't actually seen a person materialize?"

Lorenzo broke into a grin. "Rosie, do you believe in this stuff? I didn't think you went in for ghosts and poltergeists."

"Oh, she does, unfortunately," Jack said. "I'm a skeptic myself. I always think there are rational explanations for psychic phenomena."

"I haven't seen anyone materialize, no," Molly said, chuckling. "I haven't been that lucky. Or, maybe I'm just not sensitive enough. I think there has to be some special connection in order for us to see into the spirit world. But, enough of that," she said, "I think I hear my husband's car in the driveway. He can tell you more about this spirit stuff than I can."

In a moment the front door opened and a tall man with gray wavy hair brushed straight back, wearing a rumpled blue suit and a red bow tie, walked in.

"Hello," he said, his voice booming. "Glad to see you. My name is Anderson Watts, but you can call me Andy. Welcome to my home."

His wife introduced the visitors to Andy, and he shook their hands with a firm, strong grip.

He sat down at the table and told them he was a History Professor at the University of Pennsylvania, and that his specialty was American History, specifically the Revolutionary War.

"So, you see that I am in the right place," he said, his hearty laugh ringing through the kitchen. "Philadelphia is crawling with Revolutionary War battle sites. Why, the Battle of Germantown was fought only a mile from here. You can pick ten people at random in a store on Germantown Avenue and five of them will have had ancestors who fought in the war. Philadelphians tend to stay close to their roots, and this neighborhood is no exception."

"They're stuck in the past," Jack said. "That's a disadvantage of living here. Things seem more fluid, more progressive, on the West Coast. I don't mean to belittle your profession, Andy, but I'm more concerned with the future than the past."

"He's a futurist," Lorenzo said. "His job is to predict the future."

"Yes, and he acts like it's the only thing anyone should think about," Rosie said. "You know, he has an actual distaste for the past. He'd like to forget about it entirely."

Andy Watts laughed again. "Well, it's a good thing for me that you don't run a university, my friend. We History professors would be out of a job. Although, the trend is moving away from the liberal arts anyway. All the kids want these days is to learn about computers. They're focused on things like Computer Engineering."

"Good for them," Jack said. "Computers are going to revolutionize the world. Those students are making the right choice."

"But you can't escape the past," Andy said. "It's always with us, and we all have a connection to people we've never met. We are the product of their choices, their hopes and dreams and mistakes. We can't get away from them, in a way."

"Oh, don't start lecturing them, Andy," Molly said. "I'm sure they didn't come here to hear one of your lectures about the value of history. Now, why don't you show them around the house? That's what they're here for."

"Right," Andy said. "But first, let me give you a little history as background. This house was built in 1880 by the Lancasters. There's an older section, a pre-Revolutionary War set of rooms, but the bulk of it was built by the Lancaster family in 1880. The Lancasters owned it till the Depression hit, and then it was sold to another WASP family, the Penningtons. They lived here till the 1950s, then sold it to a man named Jacob Greenway, a real estate mogul. He did a lot of work on it, made some additions and renovations, but he had a respect for the original house and he didn't change it too much. He owned it for ten years, then it had two other owners before we bought it ten years ago. So, which of these families are you people related to?"

149

"My great uncle and grandmother were Lancasters," Jack said.

Andy chuckled. "Well, then you probably know more about this place than I do. What do you know?"

"Very little," Jack said. "It's a long story, but my mother's birth was, ah, hushed up. She was raised by a cousin and didn't know the connection to the Lancasters for many years. Then when she found out, she didn't tell me till the end of her life. I got a box of mementos from her, but not much else."

"Ah, yes, these people had a lot of secrets," Andy said. "We forget, but they were Victorians, and they didn't like confronting the darker side of life. They put those aspects of their lives in the closet. So, are you the only one with a connection to the house?" he said.

"My grandmother worked here as a servant," Rosie said. "She was an immigrant from Ireland, and she did domestic work here. My grandfather too. They met here, is what I was told."

"Oh, that happened a lot," Andy said. "I've done some research into the Irish immigration to this country in the late 19th century. There were millions of Irish girls who came over and got jobs in the great houses of the East Coast. And men, too, although there weren't as many opportunities for them. A common job for them was to be a coachman, a driver of the horses."

"So, it's like an 'Upstairs-Downstairs' story," Molly said. "Your ancestors came from different social classes, and they lived in different parts of the house than the Lancaster family."

"Yes," Rosie said. "That's true. But then my grandmother married one of the Lancasters, later in life."

"Oh, that happened a lot too," Andy said, chuckling. "You had all these Irish girls in close quarters with their employers, and sometimes people fell in love. It's only natural. There have been some excellent books written on that. I'm trying to remember the titles."

Molly came around to his chair and put her hand on his shoulder. "I don't think they want to hear about the books that were written about the subject," she said, gently. "I think they'd like to see where their ancestors lived."

"Of course," Andy said. "Sorry, I get long-winded sometimes. That's an occupational hazard with History professors. Anyway, let's have a tour of the old place, shall we?"

He pushed back his chair and started in the kitchen, which he said had the same black and white and green linoleum floor as when the house was built. "There have been a lot of changes and things updated," he said, "but this floor is the original."

Then he proceeded to the parlor, which was a little room off the main foyer. "This would have been where the adults would have received visitors," Andy said. "Children were not allowed here. Women would sit and drink tea with their friends. There would probably have been a little spinet piano and some uncomfortable chairs and a couch, and paintings on the walls, an Oriental rug perhaps."

Rosie got a sudden chill, and she shivered.

"What's the matter?" Jack said. "Are you okay?"

"Something happened here," Rosie said. "Something bad."

CHAPTER NINETEEN

What do you mean by that?" Jack said, raising an eyebrow. "Is this one of your psychic moments?"

"Can you describe it?" Andy said. He seemed more respectful of Rosie's intuition, and looked at her thoughtfully.

"I, I don't know," Rosie said. "I can't put a finger on it. It's a feeling, a presence. Something dark."

She looked around the room. She felt a sense of panic, confusion, voices near and far. One was an Irish voice, a man's. Was it her grandfather? She didn't remember what his voice sounded like that one time she met him as a child. This voice was full of panic, fear, a sense of being trapped.

Trapped. That was it, there was something trapped here. She looked around the room. What was it? What had happened here?

"Did you say this was sort of a formal room?" she said. "The servants wouldn't be allowed in here?"

"No," Andy said, holding a hand to his chin like a professor pondering a question from a student. "There would normally be no reason to have a servant in here. They'd come in to clean the room, dust the furniture, but not to socialize. Why?"

"I feel such anxiety here. Such fear. It's very disturbing." Rosie felt her heart beating faster, and her breath was coming in short, shallow bursts.

"Something must have happened here," Molly said. "I've felt that presence here too sometimes. A sense like the walls are closing in."

"Yes, that's it," Rosie said. "It's claustrophobic."

"Perhaps one of your relatives was called in here to be reprimanded," Molly said. "That happened a lot, you know. The Irish servants could be sent back home at any time. They lived in fear of getting fired, and if that happened no other family would hire them. Then their dream of making money and sending it home would be ruined."

"That must have been a terrible anxiety for those poor folks," Lorenzo said. "They came here to get away from the poverty in the old country. To be threatened with going back would have been a horrible thing. What would make the employers do that?"

"Oh, they thought the immigrants were low class people," Andy said. "The Irish immigrants were country people, you know, not educated. They didn't know the social graces. So, these wealthy people felt they had to watch them, that their morals weren't as good. They were afraid of the servants stealing, mostly. But there were also a lot of pregnancies among the servants. A lot of surprises, if you know what I mean. And sometimes it involved a son or daughter of the employer's family."

Rosie felt a blinding flash behind her eyeballs, and a sound like a thunderclap. She took a step backward, then sat down on the nearest chair. She started to shiver, and she couldn't stop shaking. Her teeth chattered like she was in the middle of a blizzard.

"What's the matter?" Jack said. "Rosie, what's the matter?"

"It was my grandfather in this room," Rosie said, suddenly seeing with utter clarity what had happened. "I know it now. He was called in and reprimanded because my grandmother was pregnant, and they weren't married. I can feel it. It's like a pain in this room, a shard of ice that split his heart."

"Oh, my," Molly said. "I do feel you're right. I have felt anger and pain in this room. And sometimes late at night I've heard the cry of a baby."

"You know, it's a strange thing," Andy said, clearing his throat, then his voice drifting off. "What is?" Molly said.

He looked stunned, and he was blinking his eyes furiously as if he were wrestling with a thought.

"What was your grandmother's name?" he said, to Rosie.

"It was Morley," she said. "Rose Morley."

"Oh," he said. "Then never mind."

"Andy, stop being so mysterious," Molly said. "I hate it when you get those mysterious expressions and your voice trails off like that. What are you thinking of?"

"It's nothing," he said. "I don't know if you even remember, dear, but when we first moved in and were renovating this place, I found a steamer trunk in a dark corner of the basement."

"I remember," Molly said. "There were some old pictures of the previous owners, some newspapers, moldy old books and papers. I don't recall anything that I thought was interesting, although I don't have the same fascination as you do with old, musty things."

"Well, I found it extremely interesting," Andy said. "I'm just that way, I'm afraid. I'm sure somebody threw all that stuff in a trunk and thought it was just junk, but to me it was a treasure chest. I do remember there were some letters, and one in particular, seemed to be about an Irish serving girl who got in a family way. It was a letter from her relatives in Ireland. But it was a different name, not Morley."

"Well, my grandmother's maiden name was Sullivan," Rosie said.

"Really?" Andy said, his eyes lighting up. "Good Lord, I think that's the name on the letter."

Rosie's heart leaped. "You have a letter from my grandmother?"

"Not from her, to her," Andy said. "It was written by her sister in Ireland, if I recall. I haven't looked at it in ages. I was thinking of donating it to the Balch Museum of ethnic history here in Philadelphia, but I just never got around to it."

"Well, where is it?" Molly said. "You have this poor girl on pins and needles. Can you find it?"

"Yes, I know where it is," Andy said. "In the library. Follow me."

Andy led the way down a long hallway, past large rooms filled with old pictures and antiques, including a big dining room with a stone fireplace and wood wainscoting and large windows that let in the evening light. Next was the library, a room paneled in walnut, where he proudly displayed his own collection of leather bound history books.

"I have some first editions," he said. "But I don't collect books for their monetary value. I collect what I like, and I read them over and over. There are books in here by some of the most eminent historians of the last 200 years."

"Oh, Andy, we don't need a lecture about your history books," Molly said. "I'm sure they're all gems, but you have everyone in a fever of curiosity right now, and you simply must satisfy us. Where is the letter?"

"Let me see," Andy said. "I put it in a volume by the great Irish historian D.A. Binchy." He scanned the shelves, looking for the volume. "Ah, here it is." He reached up and pulled down a thick red volume with gold lettering on the spine. He paged through it, mumbling to himself. "Amazing work, truly incisive writing," and similar comments. Finally, when Rosie was about to scream with impatience, he said, "Yes, here it is, just where I left it." He pulled out two yellowed pieces of paper, unfolded them, and gave them to Rosie. "Do you recognize the name?" he said.

Rosie had to sit down, because her knees were trembling. "Yes," she said. "It's from my great aunt Theresa, my grandmother's sister."

November, 1888

Dear Rose:

I am writing this letter with Father sitting at my elbow, by the light of the peat fire, and your sister Annie and brother Brian are with me also.

Father wants you to know how ashamed he is of you. We received word last week, through a letter from Mary Driscoll, that you have committed a most serious sin by having relations with a man before you were married. Mary told us in her letter that you did a shameful thing with a man who was employed at the same house as you, and that you had a child with him. She said you were let go by your employer because of this, and that although you are married to the man now, you were not when you became pregnant with his child.

This is something we never expected of you, Rose. It has brought shame on the family, especially now that we have found out that Mary Driscoll has told others. Only last Sunday, when we came out of church after Mass, old Mrs. Langan wagged her head and made a comment to Father about how so many of our Irish youth have gone to America and lost their morals. We all understood that she was talking about you.

It is lucky that Mother is not alive to hear this, for as mad as she was in her later years, she still had sense enough in her to be horrified at this state of affairs. You were not raised this way, Rose Sullivan, and we all think it must be the evil influence of that country you are in, where we have heard that people have all sorts of modern ideas, like men and women going to music halls together.

Do you not remember your Faith, Rose? You know that we went every Sunday to Mass in town, and Mother made sure the priests taught us well. She never got so touched in the head that she forgot her Rosary; she had it on her the day she died. Have you

157

became like so many of our countrymen and women, who went to America only to lose their Catholic Faith?

This is not what we expected when you left to go to America. You said you were only going to earn some money to send back to us, and although you have done that, it is now almost ten years since you left, and you do not seem anxious to return to us.

Now I suppose you will never come back to your home, since you have a child and a husband in America.

It gives us great pain to hear these things about you, Rose. Father is so upset he can barely keep his wits about him, and I have come upon him a few times in the fields with the tears streaming down his face. Times have been hard enough, with bad harvests and the death of our dear Mother, without you adding to his burden.

It cannot be tolerated, Rose. Father has told me to write these words: You are no longer a part of our family. You have brought shame upon us, and for that you must be banished from us. Father will not speak of you again; you are dead to him. I will say it again, to be clear: you are no longer a part of this family. Please do not write to us ever again, and you are not welcome to visit.

Just to be certain, I want to repeat that Father, Brian and Annie are all sitting here with me while I write this, and they are all in agreement. This will be the last you hear from us.

Goodbye, Rose.

God be with you.

Theresa Sullivan

Rosie put the letter down with tears in her eyes. It was as if a deep well of sadness had opened up inside her, and she was drowning in it. She understood for the first time something of the pain and anguish her grandmother felt. To be banished from her family and homeland forever! It must have been a terrible heartache for her grandmother. She remembered the old woman would never talk about her childhood in Ireland. Rosie used to try to get her to tell stories from her childhood, but the old woman's mouth would set in a thin, hard line and she'd say, "Ah, there's no point in that. All in the past, all in the past."

Now she understood. It was just too painful; the wound was still there even 70 years later.

Jack leaned down and put his hand on her shoulder. "Are you all right, Rosie?" he said. The concern in his eyes was genuine; he seemed disturbed by how upset she was. Suddenly she stood up and threw her arms around him, and sobbed into his shoulder.

Jack seemed taken aback, though he put his hand on her shoulder and patted it gently, but he had a puzzled expression on his face and he didn't seem to know what to do.

"Why don't we go back to the kitchen and sit down?" Molly said. "Andy can show your friends the rest of the house."

"Yes," Rosie said. "That's fine. You go ahead, Jack."

She let Molly take her back to the kitchen, and she sat down in the sunny kitchen, still clutching the letter, and listened to the sound of cars passing outside the window. Molly seemed to know not to talk too much, and she bustled about making a fresh cup of tea, while Rosie calmed herself down.

Finally, she sat down next to Rosie and poured a steaming cup of peppermint tea, and Rosie took a sip, letting the sweet flavor wash down her throat. Molly smiled, letting Rosie have the space to talk whenever she needed to.

"I felt her presence," Rosie finally said. "My grandmother. I think she wanted me to read that letter. So I would know the pain she felt."

Molly shook her head. "I know. I'm sure that's what it was. My husband claims to be agnostic about these things, but I believe there are spirits in this house. You know, he loves history, and he's not averse to telling a good ghost story, and we've even gone on ghost tours of some of the grand houses in Chestnut Hill, but he doesn't really believe. It's all just an entertainment for him. I'm different about that."

"I've had dreams, intuitions, strange things that have happened my whole life," Rosie said. "I've always felt like I had one foot in another world."

"Was your grandmother psychic?" Molly said.

"I think so," Rosie said. "I mean, she didn't say much about it, but I remember her telling me she had strange dreams and visions once. It was near the end of her life. I think she'd kept it inside for so long, not wanting to admit it. She told me once that her mother, my great-grandmother, had gone mad back in Ireland. She said her mother was always talking about the spirit world, talking to the air and singing strange songs. I think she didn't want to turn out like that."

"It can be a scary thing," Molly said. "You probably feel like you could get sucked in by forces not under your control, and then you wouldn't be able to get back."

Rosie sighed. "The universe is a strange place, isn't it?"

"Oh, yes," Molly said. "Exceedingly strange, I'd say."

"I felt all her pain," Rosie said. "All her loneliness and sadness. It was soul wrenching. Now I understand her better."

"And that's why you came here today," Molly said. "See, what I believe is that we're all working things out, no matter if it's in this world or another. We have work to do, and it involves connections that go down through the ages. Connections with people who went before, and people who come after us. We're all linked in one big chain. There's always a reason for what we do, or where we find ourselves. We may not understand it, but there's definitely a reason."

Rosie knew she was right, in a strange way. She felt a stronger connection to her grandmother Rose than she ever had before. She even had a picture in her mind of what her crazy great-grandmother looked like, the one who talked to fairies and saw visions.

"So, you think somehow I was supposed to come here today?" Rosie said.

"Yes," Molly said. "I do. Your grandmother was calling you here. This was all supposed to happen. Maybe now she'll be at peace."

"Yes," Rosie said. "And maybe I'll be at peace, too."

"I don't know," Molly said. "That's the work that you need to do, to find peace. You probably have some things to work out in your life."

Rosie thought of Pete, all the heartache and anger she'd had in her relationship with him. I have to make things right with him, she thought. To heal things. That's the work I have to do.

"I know one thing you should do," Molly said. "You should do psychic readings. I think you have an extraordinary sensitivity to the spirit world. You're in tune with it, and I think you should use that gift to help people. So many people are lost these days. You could help them find some peace."

"Me?" Rosie said, laughing. "Oh, I don't know." But in her heart she knew Molly was right. She'd felt different her whole life, hearing strange music and dreaming strange dreams, and maybe she did have a gift. It was something to think about.

Before long Andy led the group down the back stairs and into the kitchen. Jack's eyes looked worried when he saw her, and Rosie saw the love in them.

"Are you all right?" he said, coming over to her. "You were pretty upset."

"I'm fine now," Rosie said. "Just some spirit workings, that's all."

CHAPTER TWENTY

December 24, 1999

Three inches of snow had fallen earlier, but by evening the sky was clear and filled with millions of stars. The shops of New Hope were closed for the holiday, and people were mostly inside getting ready for their dinners. The cold, clear water of the Delaware River reflected the color and sparkle from the stores and restaurants hung with Christmas lights on both sides of the waterway.

Rosie heard laughter from the restaurant downstairs, and she was happy at the sound of conviviality. She was always delighted to welcome people into her restaurant, and on any other night she would have been down there chatting with the diners, perhaps getting up on stage to sing later in the evening, although she didn't do that now as much as she used to. Her voice had gotten huskier with age, and it was harder to hit the high notes these days.

Tonight, though, she was hosting a Christmas Eve dinner for her family, and she had had the chef prepare a lovely repast, with turkey, ham and even a steak for Pete, who liked red meat, and plenty of side dishes. Pete and Betty were due to arrive any minute, and Jack was in the bathroom shaving, getting ready for the evening. He was whistling a tune that he always whistled when he was feeling buoyant, which was "Happy" by the Rolling Stones.

It was an exciting time, because Rosalie, Pete's daughter, was home from her freshman year of college, and Marty, her 16-year-old brother, was coming with his latest girlfriend. He was a handsome boy with a great singing voice and loads of confidence, and he seemed to attract girls as easy as breathing.

163

In another week it would be the turn of the millennium, and Rosie was amazed that she was around for it. She'd never thought she would lived to be 50, let alone 72, which what she was on her last birthday. She hadn't expected to be here for the dawn of a new century, but here it was.

She looked out the window at the bookshop down the street that had been owned by Mercy and Lorenzo. Lorenzo had died only two years ago, at the age of 95, a white haired old man who still woke up every day looking for reasons to be happy. He worked a few hours a day in the bookshop right up until the end, chatting with customers about philosophy, art, films, music -- all of his loves. He told everyone who'd listen that he was the luckiest man alive, since he'd met Mercy, his soul mate, late in life and had twenty years with her. "Twenty, imagine that!" he'd say. "Life has many surprises waiting for us." Lorenzo had taught Rosie a lot about how to live a happy life, how to look for the little miracles every day and not get caught up in worry or anxiety.

There were so many people worrying now about something called Y2K, which was going to happen on New Year's Eve when all the computers had to switch their dates to the year 2000. It was supposed to trigger a mass computer shutdown, and global chaos, because the computers hadn't been programmed correctly years ago and they couldn't reset themselves to the year 2000.

Pete, who worked as a software engineer now, since Jack had gotten him into the industry when he came back from Ireland ten years ago, was of the opinion that there would be a global panic and a descent into chaos with millions of computers crashing. He had already stocked his house in Bucks County with bottled water and food in case the food supply chain was broken, he had a generator in case his electricity went out, and he had everything he needed to keep his family safe.

Jack, by contrast, was not as pessimistic. "It's a big fuss about nothing," he said. "Really, it's not going to affect that many people. The big computer systems, the ones that run everything important, have been reprogrammed. There's nothing to worry about."

That was Jack, though, the natural optimist. He seemed to see the bright side of everything and he freely admitted it was part of his strategy for living. "Being an optimist makes you healthier, in the long run," he'd say. "And I want to be alive to see all the great changes that are coming."

It did seem like a lot of his predictions were coming true. The things he'd told Rosie almost twenty years ago when they'd met were either here or on the horizon. Cell phones. Fax machines. Better health care. Industrial robots. Microwave ovens. Personal computers. And the giant global network that connected them, that was getting more powerful all the time and connecting people in new and different ways. The next thing, the thing he was really excited about now, was artificial intelligence. "It's going to happen, Rosie," he'd say. "It's coming. There are research labs now where they're getting close. There will be a time when we can talk to computers the same way we talk to people. They will have brains and whatever else you want to call it -- souls? Then, there will come a time when the computers are smarter than us, and that's when we'll discover the secrets of the universe."

Rosie would laugh and tell him he was being poetic again, even though he claimed not to like poetry.

She was still not sure about the computer revolution. It seemed that these machines were taking over more and more of people's lives. She missed the days when people sat around and talked to each other instead of to their screens. She looked over at the bedroom door, and even though it was closed she could see the blue glow from the computer screen coming out the bottom of the door. They've made their way into people's bedrooms, she thought. Nobody would have predicted that 20 years ago. What's next?

Rosie preferred her psychic work. She had become known around town for her psychic abilities, and even though she'd never opened her own shop, she would often do readings for people in a room at the back of the restaurant. She had learned to read tea leaves, tarot cards, and a scrying ball, but her real talent was in communicating with the dead. Ever since the incident at the Lancasters' house in Chestnut Hill she had decided to let her abilities come out, and it had been a wonderful and strange adventure. She often saw spirits when she did a reading, and she learned to figure out what they were trying to tell her. She saw them more clearly now, to the point that she sometimes mistook a spirit for a "real" person. Once, she saw a woman in a black dress and a bonnet sitting at a table in the restaurant late at night when she was closing up, and she called out, "Excuse me, but we're closed now," before she realized it was a spirit. When she approached the table the woman smiled at her, then disappeared.

"We're certainly a pair," Jack would say. "The spirit woman, who talks to people from the past, and the tech guru, who thinks only of the future. "It's perfect! That's why we should get married."

He had been asking her to marry him for years, and Rosie always said no. It's not that she didn't love him; it was that she had a deep fear of marriage, and she didn't think it worked for her. "I have 'marriage phobia'", she'd say. "And I haven't found a way to get over it."

There was a knock on the door, and she ran to it excitedly, hearing the voices of Pete and Betty and their children. She opened the door and saw Pete, dressed in his ever present blue jeans and flannel shirt, his hair gray at the temples but a big smile wreathing his face, and Betty, looking as beautiful as ever in a tasteful maroon dress, pearls, and a shawl of a Logan green color that set off her hazel eyes and caramel skin. Her hair was jet black and swept away from her face, setting off her high cheekbones. She looked confident and successful, a look befitting the fact that she was now a partner in a high-powered law firm.

Then came Rosalie, who had a combination of Pete and Betty's looks. She was a slim girl of 19 who had long limbs that she moved with the grace of a ballerina. She had Betty's caramel skin and Pete's pouty mouth and shy smile. She liked to talk with Rosie about the psychic world, and Rosie saw in her a kindred spirit.

Then came Marty. He seemed to be lit from within, with an electric energy that almost warmed you when you were near him. He had black curly hair, green eyes, and pale skin, a chiseled jaw and a lean, angular body. His smile, though, was like a blessing. It lit up a room. He was magnetic, and seemed to draw people to him. He was only 16, but he already carried himself with the confidence of an adult. He was a talented musician, and had a guitar with him, so Rosie knew he was planning on playing some songs later.

Rosie welcomed them all, took their coats and hats and told them to go and fix themselves drinks, while she put the dinner out.

Jack came and helped her, and she felt a profound happiness listening to their voices, all chattering away at once.

167

There was a fire burning in the big stone fireplace in the bar area, and Christmas carols playing on the sound system. The smell of food filled the air. Jack's presence was calming, and Rosie felt like this was one of the happiest moments of her life. *Funny that it took me this long to experience true happiness,* she thought. *I guess I learn slowly.*

At dinner, the conversation was full of laughter and good spirits. Rosie looked at her family, the people who came from her, and felt the presence of her ancestors. She could see hints of her parents and her grandmother Rose in them, and even what she knew of her grandfather Peter, she felt that his magnetism, his charisma, was evident in Marty.

And James Charlesworth, too. He was there also. Pete had the curve of his jaw, the stubborn mouth, the reserved demeanor. And through him, Rosalie had some of that quiet strength and stillness.

Charlesworth was gone now. She'd had a phone call from him five years before, when he said he was dying of cancer and he wanted to say goodbye. He sounded old, tired, on a scratchy phone connection. There was still something in his voice, though, that compelled her, touched her. She choked up, thinking of the love she had felt for him all those decades ago.

"I still love you, Rosie," he said, in his whispery, old man's voice. "I have never forgotten you all these years. There's not an hour that has gone by where I have not thought of you with fondness. I wish things had turned out differently."

"We made mistakes," Rosie replied, "but we can't torture ourselves about them. I was just a girl, and you were far away from your family, during a war. We did what we needed to do to survive.

168

And, in the end, something good came of it, James. We produced Pete, and now he has two beautiful children. None of that would have happened without us."

"Yes," he said, after a pause. "You're right. It's another good memory for me, meeting Pete in Ireland. He's a fine young man. You should be proud of him."

"So should you, James," Rosie said.

That was the last time she'd spoken to him. A month later she'd gotten a letter from him.

She had saved the letter for five years, and now the time was right to show it to Pete.

"Pete, can you come with me for a minute?" she said, then led him into the office where Jack had his computers. She sat him sit down in one of the leather office chairs, then handed him the letter.

December, 1994

Rosie

By the time you read this I will be gone. I have instructed my solicitor to send this to you after my passing. I called you today, and I am grateful that I was able to speak with you. I didn't know if you would refuse to have a conversation with me.

I have been revisiting the past quite a bit lately, and I feel the need apologize to you for all the mistakes I made. I'm afraid I made some terrible decisions over the years, and I have regretted them immensely.

I feel that I should have stayed with you in America when the war ended. It was a cowardly thing to run back to England the way I did. In my defense, I thought I had a position to maintain, an image of propriety, perhaps an expectation to meet a certain standard of behavior among the people of my country and class.

It was an artificial construct, a tissue of lies, however. I married my wife Annabelle simply because it was the expected thing in our little corner of the world. She came from the right family, she had the right amount of money and breeding, and it was the natural course of things for us to get married. We had a good marriage by all outward appearances, but it was a sham. Annabelle and I were never really in love. We lived parallel lives that never intersected.

I realized as the years went on that the only true love I ever had was for you. When I met you again in London in the 1960s I felt like I had been given a second chance, and I wanted so much for things to work out between us. I cannot tell you how much that meant to me. I used to wake up every morning thinking of the next time I'd get to see you, and the time I spent with you made me feel more alive than any other time in my life.

For a brief period, I thought we had a chance to rekindle the flame. I would have given up everything for you then. My other life seemed shallow and sad without you. Do you remember when I came to Ireland with you? You wanted to see your grandmother's birthplace, and it seemed to move you in a profound way. You looked so beautiful then, so fragile too, and I wanted to hold you and protect you for the rest of our lives. I wanted so badly to come with you when you left for America.

Alas, you did not feel the same way. You had moved on, I suppose. It was devastating for me, and I never really got over it. I mourned you for years afterward. Oh, I went about the business of my life the same as always, but inside I was shattered, broken. I had lost the one big love of my life.

I have been a good father to my children, and a dutiful husband to my wife. I had a good career in the intelligence service, and all in all it was a well-lived life. But there was always something missing, a hole inside that could never be filled. Annabelle could never fill it, I am afraid. She is gone now, and she died without finding out about the great love I had for you. It is better, I know, that she did not.

I must confess that I followed you from afar after you left. I worked in intelligence, after all, and I could not resist using my contacts in America to keep tabs on you. I know that you had a career on the fringes of the music industry, and that you never married. I followed Pete also, although I must admit I missed his involvement with the IRA until you called me.

I hope you don't find this revelation distasteful. I just couldn't let go of you. I couldn't let you walk out of my life and just disappear. Perhaps it was wrong, but I needed to know about you.

And that brings me to the important part of this letter. I knew you were always curious about your Irish roots, and so I did some research about them. Looking into people's backgrounds was my life for so many years, and I was good at it.

Anyway, when I looked into your genealogy I found something very interesting. I learned that a man named Sean McCarthy was suspected of murdering a British officer in 1880. You may not know this name, but I will explain its significance.

171

The murder was in a barracks in the midlands of Ireland. I will get back to that later. Before that, however, I need to tell you about Mary Driscoll. She was your grandmother's cousin, and she came from the same town, Skibbereen. They emigrated to America together in 1880 and worked as servants in the same household in Pittsburgh for a time.

Mary had a very different life than your grandmother. She eventually married an Irish immigrant who became wealthy from his construction business, and she died a rich woman, at the age of 90. Toward the end of her life Mary wrote a memoir and paid to have it printed. It will not win any awards for literary skill, but it is a lively account of what it was like to be an immigrant in America in the late 19th and early 20 centuries. Mary donated the book along with a lot of her papers, to the Balch Institute for Ethnic Studies in Philadelphia, which has an extensive collection of materials related to immigration.

I tracked the memoir down through my channels, and I had someone send me copies of the early chapters. In it Mary refers to her village of Skibbereen, and her friend Rose Sullivan, and talks of a handsome boy named Sean McCarthy who Rose met the night before they left for America.

That name "Sean McCarthy" triggered something in my memory. Years before, just to satisfy my curiosity, I had read through the military reports surrounding my grandfather James Charlesworth's death. You may remember me mentioning that he had died in a skirmish with some rebels in Ireland in the late 19th century. Well, when I found the records it turned out that particular story was a family myth. I found to my surprise that he had been murdered in cold blood, and the culprit had never been found.

There was a suspect, though. Several soldiers who were stationed there said they'd seen a local boy, a lad who sold vegetables, taken into Lieutenant Charlesworth's quarters by a sergeant who suspected him of selling poteen, or moonshine. They said the boy's name was Sean McCarthy. He disappeared after that, and so the case was closed after a time.

The same Sean McCarthy? Well, that is impossible to prove more than a century later, of course. I'm sure there were other Sean McCarthys in the Ireland of that time. I searched and searched, but I could turn up no connections, no links. It's very probable that he left Ireland in a hurry, because the penalties were severe for the murder of an English officer. He would have been shot, for certain.

The interesting thing is that in Mary Driscoll's book she says a man looking very like Sean McCarthy turned up in Philadelphia soon after Mary and Rose moved there, in the mid-1800s. He was a handsome Irishman, and he had a beautiful singing voice, which Mary remembered as sounding very much like Sean McCarthy's. This man called himself Peter Morley, though, and he eventually married Rose Sullivan.

There is no more mention of him or Rose, for that matter, in Mary's book. Mary and Rose's lives diverged, and that episode is just a minor incident in her book. But it's a tantalizing question: was Peter Morley really Sean McCarthy?

We'll never know, of course, but if he was, then he could have been the murderer of my grandfather.

Which means that you and I have a connection that goes back to the past, to our ancestors in the Ireland of the 19th century. I never gave much credence to the psychic world that you felt so close to, Rosie, but I do think this is an amazing fact. If the Sean

173

McCarthy who killed my grandfather was the same as your grandfather, then maybe we are connected on some spiritual level that we never guessed at. Do you think that is possible? I would believe almost anything now. I am close to the end of my life, Rosie, and I am full of questions about the hereafter. Why are we here? What is our purpose? What do our lives mean? What are we here to learn?

We will never know if the Sean McCarthy who killed my grandfather is the same man who married your grandfather. That is a question that is lost to time, I am afraid. I cannot stop thinking about it, though.

I lay awake at night and think of these things. I have read many books on religion in the last year, and sometimes I wonder about the concept of reincarnation. Do you think our souls are born again, Rosie? Do you think that we were lovers in another life? Do you think we will be lovers in the next life? Somehow that comforts me, to think that we might meet again.

I have only a little while to live, my doctor tells me. There is something I want to do before I die, however. I am enclosing a cheque made out to you. It is a sum of 50,000 pounds. I would like you to give the money to our son, Pete. It is not enough to pay for all the years that he has not had a father, but think of it as a gift that he can use for his children. Perhaps he can pay something toward their college education with it.

I have instructed my solicitor to give a letter to my children at the probate of my estate, which will explain our relationship to them. I did not want Annabelle to know, but since she is gone I think I would like my sons and daughter to know something of my inner life. I hope to meet you again, Rosie.

Goodbye.

James

While Pete read the letter Rosie sat and thought about the strangest things. She looked out and saw the light of the moon and the Christmas lights reflecting off the waters of the river. Rosie thought of another river, so long ago, the Schuykill, where she'd told James about the child she was carrying. That day had been so traumatic when he'd told her he was going back to England that he was not going to marry her and stay in Philadelphia. Later that day she'd stood on a bridge spanning the river and had almost jumped into the swirling water below, until a ruddy faced Irish policeman had pulled her down and talked her out of her mad plan.

If that policeman hadn't come along the next 50 years of my life wouldn't have happened, Rosie thought. Pete wouldn't be here, nor his children. Nor Jack. It was a sobering thought, but one that made her somehow feel protected. Maybe there's someone up there watching out for me.

After Pete finished the letter from James he fell silent. He seemed to fill up for a moment, and he looked out the window to compose himself.

"Am I like him?" he asked, after a time.

"Yes," Rosie said. "You are like him in a lot of ways. You have a sharp mind, and you are reserved like he was. You keep things close to your chest. You have the same expression around the mouth, as if you're trying to keep from saying certain things. You have his kindness, though. He was a kind man, in spite of everything. He was just trapped in his life, and couldn't get out."

175

"He helped me twice when I was trapped," Pete said. "He got me out of Nam and then out of Northern Ireland. Both times I could have died. I owe him."

"He was just trying to make up for not being in your life for so long," Rosie said. "He wanted to make up for the damage he did to you."

"I never got to thank him," Pete said. "And now. . . what's this about a check for 50,000 pounds? What's that about?" He turned the letter over and read the date. "He sent this in 1994. Why didn't you show it to me before?"

"I decided to keep it secret because I just wanted to wait for the right time," Rosie said. " I wanted to make sure you were in a good place in your life. I knew it would come in handy some day for your children's education, but I wanted it to be the right time. This is the time, I feel. Rosalie is in college, and Marty is not far behind. I'm sure you could use it."

Pete laughed. "Use it? I sure could. Betty and I were wondering how to get the money together to put both kids through college. It was going to put a strain on our finances, that's for sure. This is a great Christmas present. I wish I could thank James."

Rosie put her hand on his. "Don't worry about it. He knew he did two good things for you. And now there's another. I'm sure he was happy to do it, knowing you had two children. It'll come in handy for you, Pete.

"And speaking of the money," she said, "there's actually a bit more. You see, I took that money and invested it in some technology stocks that Jack recommended. It did very well. You have close to $125,000 now, Pete."

Pete took a deep breath. "Really? My God, I can't believe it. This is the best Christmas I've ever had."

He threw his arms around Rosie and gave her a big hug, something he hadn't done since he was a small boy.

Rosie was touched, and felt herself trembling with joy.

"Thanks, Mom," Pete said. "Thanks for watching out for me."

"Oh, I'm not the only one watching out for you," Rosie said. "I know my Irish grandmother, Rose, is. Or maybe it's her mother. I don't know, but I have a feeling of peace sometimes, like we're being taken care of."

"Well, this is certainly going make my family happy," Pete said. "Can we go tell the others? I'd sure like to see the look on Betty's face when we tell her we have the kids' college tuitions taken care of."

"Sure," Rosie said. "Let's go tell them."

Betty screamed and gave Rosie a hug when she found out. Rosalie and Marty jumped up and down and clapped, and Jack sat back and smiled. He seemed to enjoy these family gatherings at least as much as Rosie did. He didn't have much family of his own, and he always said that Rosie should appreciate her family more, because it was such a precious thing.

Later they sang Christmas carols around the beautiful tree with all the lights and decorations, next to a fire in the big stone fireplace, and Rosie put her head on Jack's shoulder and felt utterly at peace.

"Happy?" Jack said, whispering in her ear.

"Completely," she said.

"Then this is the perfect time," he said.

"For what?" she asked.

Suddenly Jack stood up and asked for silence. Pete turned off the music, and everyone gathered around Jack and Rosie.

"As you all know, I've been asking Rosie to marry me for years," Jack said. "She keeps turning me down, but I'm not a person who gives up easily. I am an optimist, someone who believes that each day has the potential to be better than the last one. I have woken up every day of the last year thinking that this day will be the one that Rosie agrees to marry me. It hasn't happened yet, but that hasn't dimmed my hope.

"Well," he continued, "I think that I'm going to try one more time. This is a special time, because as you know in a week it will be the turning of the millennium. A new century is on the horizon, and I aim to live as long as possible in it, to see as many of the coming wonders as I can. And I want my Rosie right by my side, as we stride forth confidently into this new era.

"So that's why," he went on, getting down on one knee, "I want to ask you again, Rosie Morley, for the umpteenth time, and in front of all your family, to marry me. It's Christmas Eve, the millennium turns in a week, and this is the perfect time. Plus, I have something that may persuade you."

He reached in his pocket and pulled out an antique gold ring. It had a big diamond in the middle and a beautiful pattern of intertwining ribbons of gold surrounding it. "This," he said, "is a ring that could have been worn by my grandmother Victoria Lancaster. I found it years ago in a box in my mother's attic, and I've had it appraised and it's dated at 1906. It's almost a hundred years old, and since I know you like old things, Rosie, I thought you'd like this."

He paused. "I love you with all my heart, Rosie, and I want to walk forward into the future with you alone. I want to be with you as your husband, your soul mate, your best friend. I want us to be together for eternity. I'm asking you in front of all the people who are most important to you: Will you marry me, Rosie Morley?

Rosie looked around at her family, her eyes brimming with tears, and saw their happy, expectant faces looking straight at her.

She smiled and said, "Yes."

THE END

THE END OF BOOK FIVE

This is the fifth of seven books in the Rose Of Skibbereen series. Look for the other books on Amazon at amazon.com/author/johnmcdonnell.

A word from John McDonnell:

I have been a writer all my life, but after many years of doing other types of writing I'm finally returning to my first love, which is fiction. I write in the horror, sci-fi, romance, humor and fantasy genres, and I have published 24 books on Amazon. I also write plays, and I have a YouTube channel where I post some of them. I live near Philadelphia, Pennsylvania with my wife and four children, and I am a happy man.

My books on Amazon: amazon.com/author/johnmcdonnell.

My YouTube channel:

https://www.youtube.com/user/McDonnellWrite/videos?view_as=subscriber

Look me up on Facebook at: https://www.facebook.com/JohnMcDonnellsWriting/.

Did you like this book? Did you enjoy the characters? Do you have any advice you'd like to give me? I love getting feedback on my books. Send me an email at mcdonnellwrite@gmail.com.

Find all the "Rose Of Skibbereen" books here:

amazon.com/author/johnmcdonnell.

Ingram Content Group UK Ltd.
Milton Keynes UK
UKHW041357190723
425433UK00003B/35

9 798651 501427